3/16

gift

2

"Such, according to the best information we have been able to obtain, is a faithful description of the scene that has transacted in our midst. It has given us pain to record it: but in doing so, we feel, deeply feel, that we are fulfilling a solemn duty which as one of it's members we owe to this community, and as an American citizen to our country at large. Let no one suppose that we would lightly say a word in derogation of the character of the city in which we live...

We have drawn the above gloomy and hideous picture, not for the purpose of holding it up as a fair representation of the moral condition of St. Louis... but that the immediate actors in the horrid tragedy may see the work of their hands, and shrink in horror from a repetition of it, and in humble penitence seek the forgiveness of that community whose laws they have so outraged...and that all may see, (and be warned in time) the legitimate results of the spirit of *mobism*, and whither, unless arrested in it's first outbreakings, it is sure to carry us."

-*The St. Louis Observer*, *May 3rd, 1836.*

Ugly Water

By

Joseph A. Wood

Saint Louis, Missouri

ISBN 978-1-4116-2218-0

Dedicated to the people of St. Louis County

Introduction

Americans have been said to have a fascination with violence. Indeed, in the last century we have collectively watched the theaters of war, politics, and tragedy unfold on our own television sets; we have had moments of evil etched into our memory. Think of the dates we keep: *December 7th, 1941, November 22nd, 1963, September 11th, 2001.* We mark our lives by these moments. As human beings, our common destiny is ultimately *death*, and that may explain its popular cultural significance. Despite this unique experience, we may come to find that *all* times and places have been populated with such violence. Lynching, murder, and assassination has been the subject of art, literature, history, and civilization since it's very beginning. Perhaps it is simply human nature that throughout history--men have attempted to use the instrument of violence in an attempt to right "wrongs" that cannot be righted.

The following pages document just such a story.

This small work is an attempt to isolate and frame one deleted, forgotten, whitewashed moment in our past. 1894 was one hundred years ago, and I find curious and surprising the world that occupied that moment. It is important to remember that these people are not characters who can be framed, but were once young and as alive as we are right in this moment. They can be categorized through the narrow lens of time as either black or white, good or evil, but we *must know* that they were much more, just as we are--and that most of us are kept in secret to ourselves and those few who knew us. In the end, we merely have what has survived by chance or by design, the storms and floods and whims of those who can either keep the documents, the photographs, the newspapers for new generation--or to simply throw them away on the ash heap.

Joseph Allen Wood

That is why snares are all around you,
why sudden peril terrifies you,
why it is so dark you cannot see,
and why a flood of water covers you.

"Is not God in the heights of heaven?
And see how lofty are the highest stars!
Yet you say, 'What does God know?
Does he judge through such darkness?
Thick clouds veil him, so he does not see us
as he goes about in the vaulted heavens.'

Will you keep to the old path
that evil men have trod?
They were carried off before their time,
their foundations washed away by a flood.

- *The book of Job* 22:10-16

The Ghost

*Judge Lynch has long held a prominent place in the
administration of Justice. In rough communities on
the frontier, his is often the first court to be
organized, and its rude decrees are enforced
without any delay for exceptions or appeals. Even
when an orderly administration of law has been
established, a peculiarly atrocious crime is liable to
arouse the old demand for speedy vengeance, and
the excited populace, too impatient to await the
regular processes of the courts, insist upon acting
themselves as Judge, Jury, and Executioners.*
-September 30, 1882 Leslie's Weekly

There is undoubtedly a stigma that exists
when dealing with a subject such as Lynching or
Race; a deep sense of paranoia that runs so deep,
that it really is never dealt with. Conversations on
the subject usually tend to be short, and
uncomfortable. Even saying the word, one feels a
sort of shame; it invites all sorts of dark questions
about the dark places in human curiosity. It seems
at times best left *forgotten.*

A few years ago, I was shopping at a local bookstore, gathering information for a story that I was writing, when I stumbled upon something unexpected. I had been looking for a section that dealt with the subject of lynching. With little to no luck, I had discovered that beyond photographic evidence, there is not a lot of material out there that documents or provides extensive insight into such a covert time in our past. Additionally, lynching is a touchy subject; so touchy that the "uncomfortableness" extends to most modern publishers, writers, or booksellers—who appear to try for more conservative and socially acceptable themes, lest anyone be "offended." Finding no real hard data on the subject, I resolved to make the most out of my otherwise uneventful visit to the bookstore by reading a locally marketed book about urban legends and tall tales.

The small paperback went briefly into the St. Louis past, recounting for tourists all of the stories that I had first heard long ago on school playgrounds and in trips through the woods with my childhood friends. The ghost stories of the old breweries and nineteenth-century factories that line South St. Louis were there in abundance, as well as a laundry list of haunted old mansions along the Mississippi River. As I was about to close the book, the word "lynched" caught the corner of my eye. I spent the next five minutes re-reading each page, trying to find what I had just flipped past. Then I saw it again. What followed was a two-sentence reference to a black man who had been accused of rape, and then taken to the main bridge in Valley Park, Missouri, and lynched. There were no details, no date, and no name.

I had assumed that to gain perspective on the subject of lynching, one would have to travel down south to "Dixie." St. Louis is sometimes considered by northerners a *southern city*; despite the fact that St. Louis is usually branded "Gateway to the West," we *are* perhaps the northernmost "southern city" in the United States. Having traveled as a student, I had come away with notions first-hand that both confirmed and denied what I was always told by people about the American South. I had been taught that lynchings were something that happened only in the "deep south"--Alabama, Georgia, Louisiana, or Mississippi--but not here.

It has been said that Lynching is peculiar to the United States; it is an American invention. Surely, it is safe to assume that wheresoever one might dig, they may find such a peculiarly *American* story.

I decided to dig in my own backyard.

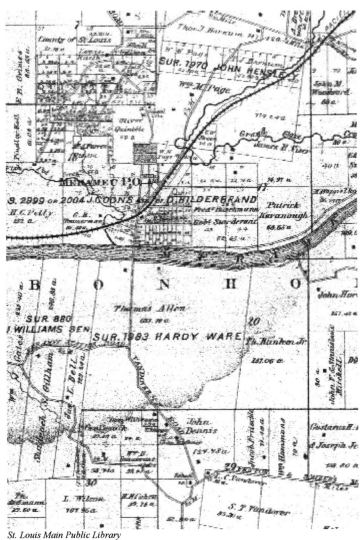

St. Louis Main Public Library

16

Valley Park

In 1909, the local newspaper The Valley Park Sun described its small river town in a special issue, aimed at celebrating its achievement and stature as a growing community of God-fearing middle class workers and churchgoers. "The Meramec River runs through Valley Park, and it is the prettiest stream for canoeing in the country," quotes the paper of an enthusiastic river-man. "It winds like a broad ribbon of alternate gold and silver thro' hills and meadows--as you glide along one finds before him a picture so tranquil and beautiful that all troublous thoughts forsake the mind and the sensation is one of keen delight."

Delight is a peculiar word to describe the forlorn town of Valley Park; a town that clings only to the river from whence it came, and also returns from time to time. The Meramec is the soothsayer of time--as it always has been, and was--back when the place seemed so tranquil. The empty streets linger along the ribbon of water, like an aging woman awaiting eternity.

The town is situated on the southern slope of a large rise just north of the Meramec River, in a hilly portion of St. Louis County that was known 100 years ago as Bonhomme Township, just about 15 miles southwest of the city of St. Louis. It is one of the oldest and yet *least* known about historic places in St. Louis County.

It was once an Indian village; known at times as Sulphur Springs, Nasby, and Meramec. Here, a man named John Dougherty first operated a ferry across the river. On February 24, 1853 the Missouri Legislature granted a charter to a small group of men to build a bridge across the Meramec River, near the Fish Pot Creek. Three years later, a grand steel arched three-truss bridge was unveiled. It would later become known affectionately by locals as the "old wagon bridge."

At the time, the new county bridge spanned majestically across the Meramec as a sign of things to come. It was. By 1890, it was the place where the St. Louis- San Francisco and the Missouri-Pacific rail lines converged. An additional bridge was built only a few hundred yards east of its sister bridge, to accommodate the Frisco railroad line.

Both the bridges and the county roads that intersected here became the main trade route that extended to a wide area in St. Louis County, with connections to Fenton, Hillsboro, Manchester, St. Charles, and the city of St. Louis--making the bridge a vital centerpiece for the Bonhomme Township, St. Louis County, and for Valley Park in general. Once the bridges went up, population and commerce steadily rose. Companies moved in.

Lots all around Valley Park were divided up into smaller pieces and sold. As the 1904 Louisiana Purchase Exposition was underway in St. Louis, plans for Valley Park were already being laid out as the future site of a great city of industry.

Gerhardt H. Timmermann, a local eccentric German immigrant who had made a large fortune manufacturing cannonballs in his St. Louis foundry during the Civil War, owned most of the land in town. He erected a large mansion just to the north of the wagon bridge, which he proposed as a site for his "Sulphur Springs Sanitarium." The curative powers of the Meramec River were widely speculated about, and Timmermann had picked up this notion from the local farmers who would go down to the banks of the river, filling barrels with "home-remedy." He was convinced that the mysterious waters of the Meramec would provide cures from various ailments of the body and mind. In his sanitarium, the curious river water would be connected through pipes to every room. After his idea failed, he sold the property off and left Valley Park. It is still said in town that one can every so often smell the sulphur in the air by the 141 bridge.

A hundred years ago, this area earned a reputation for its carnival atmosphere; a playground, whose main attraction was the river. The "Sulphur Springs Sanitarium" became "The Paddle and Saddle Club", and "Harry Arnold's Boathouse and Landing"--where not patients, but sportsmen and vacationers could unwind and relax. The resort known as the Meramec Highlands was nestled along the rail line and the Meramec between Valley Park and Kirkwood just a couple miles to the east. At the time, it was claimed that this stretch of river was more heavily navigated than a city street. For years, special excursion trains, full of families from the city and outlying areas, made dozens of stops a day here. Once the principal resort on the Meramec--old photographs of Valley Park convey another world, all to it's own satisfaction. Canoeing and yachts, avid fishermen, swimmers, and children frolicked among the landings and riverbends of the now abandoned river. These waters so densely populated with fish, now flow in silence. There are no boats, no ferries, no canoeing parties. Playgrounds such as the Highlands and Arnold's Boathouse are but a memory.

Only a few miles to the west was built the theme-park Six Flags Over Mid-America. A few miles northwest is the Museum of Transportation--commonly known to local school-children as the "Train Museum." Just due east is Laumeier Sculpture Park, where families can walk through unending fields of outdoor modern art, most notably by the great Alexander Calder. Dwarfed in between all of these childhood excursions is Valley Park. There are no landmarks; no sites; no memories in Valley Park. The icons that emerge out of the grey maze of aluminum siding and smoke all conjure images from a forgotten time: the spire of Sacred Heart Church, the old grain mill, the vintage "FRISCO" railcar, and the Frisco Railroad Bridge across the Meramec.

The main reason for its existence at all is that *it was once the heart of civilization.* Originally, the town was but a simple Post Office out in the wilderness, known as Meramec. Here, 300 settlers made the village of Meramec into the prestigious resort town of Valley Park. Today, it is merely a shadow of its former self. Driving past, you would never know its prominent place, neither as a historic landmark nor as a place of amusement.

The important thing about Valley Park is that it is a town steeped in history. Like few other towns that have somehow survived modernity, Valley Park silently celebrates its rich heritage in its own subtle dignity of personality, tradition, and architecture, out of what still remains. Though terrible flooding in the last century has washed away much of the original structures, all one has to do is drive through the center of town to see that little has changed in this community. And yet, everything has changed.

To understand Valley Park, you must understand small American towns--that somehow find ways to conservatively *evolve*, rather than destroy what once was. Anyone who has traveled the old American roads has seen the typical small-town; that has escaped each fleeting outside influence as though it were a high refuge above the flood. In today's world, Valley Park seems an island all to itself. Such God-fearing places are controlled not by passion, but by climate; by *nature*--rather than the changing fashions of time. Indeed, this town could have been anywhere in small-town America, but the people are pure Missouri.

Ironically--one hundred years ago, Valley Park seemed "ahead" of its time. On it's front page, The Valley Park Sun had in 1909 made the claim that "...we have fellow-citizens from all parts of the world, who freely exercise all of their religious, political, and social rights, without encroaching upon the privileges of other citizens differing from them in beliefs and customs." "Indeed," it says, "the great principle that all men were created free and equal seems to govern our people in their daily intercourse with each other." As to the "Colored Contingent" of Valley Park, it states, "There are about 100 colored people in the town and vicinity, and they are of the well-behaved and industrious kind, thus being good and useful citizens."

The town today is absent of its earlier diversity. If there are any number of non-white citizens that still live here--they seem to be hidden or otherwise removed from the public square. Much of Valley Park seems removed; It's parks are empty, its streets devoid of pedestrians jogging or waiting for the bus, and its wooden frame homes look weathered, but otherwise much as they did 50 years ago. Besides the ebb and flow of trucks and trains that constantly penetrate Valley Park's borders, the heart of town is serenely silent.

On Benton Street, one of the main arteries of the original grid laid out over 100 years ago, is the heart of town government and law. An old two-story brick structure that was once a schoolhouse serves as City Hall and Police Department, as well as part-time library. From here, one might imagine the Missouri artist Thomas Hart Benton getting an inspiration from the obsolete simplicity found in its environs; a Mayberry or Sparta of the real world. The large parking lot outside City Hall is usually bare of visitors, save that of the local mechanic hosing down a muddy city vehicle, or occasionally working on a broke down patrol car.

By the turn of the century, Valley Park was nearly at its peak. Though the town had blossomed, there was no official police station in Valley Park. The town was as late as 1909 not yet incorporated, and for years, it had merely relied on a Justice of the Peace to maintain order and justice. At times, the farmers and businessmen of Valley Park would have to depend on the aid of lawmen in the nearby town of Manchester, or in the County seat of Clayton. Other than a routine outburst of public drunkenness, or the occasional brawl, law and order largely presided *itself* over the majority of the citizens of St. Louis County. "...[C]rime of a serious or criminal character is less frequent than in a majority of incorporated towns or cities," stated the town's newspaper in 1909. "The chief reason for this desirable condition is that our people are peaceable and law-abiding, and, besides, the law *is rigidly enforced when it becomes necessary.*"

The Cause

The history of lynching in the United States is a bloody record that began after the Civil War and started to vanish sometime in the late 1950's. That is not to say that there were no lynchings before this period—we happen to know that there were. We simply have *no record* of them. The thousands of men and women that were hung or burned alive in this period are unknown to us, and are but a dizzying list of names and dates that go on and on and on.

Mob law and mob justice go back to the earliest times. Lynchings are but one of the latest forms of *mobism* in human history. In the short history of the United States, lynching has been responsible for the deaths of at least 5,000 Americans. Many elderly citizens can yet remember a day when it was still a common practice. Racism, as both a cause and effect of the institutions of American Slavery and Jim Crow, found in their administration a useful and powerful symbol in lynching. Though it is most noted in association with its racial application in the last century, *lynching is one of the earliest forms of terrorism that was practiced in the New World.*

A lynching could consist of any form of murder; shooting, beating, dismembering--but it's most common form came in burning or hanging the victim. Contrary to popular belief, lynchings were not confined to the American South. In the time after the Civil War, hangings became synonymous with the vigilante law of the "Wild West," and were carried out in town squares, college campuses, farmer's fields, and under bridges--all across the United States. While some may have seemed as orderly as a state execution, others were downright diabolical and savage in nature. Often, death was not the only aim of the lynching party. Instruments of torture sometimes consisted of sticks, ice picks, saws, and even gallons of gasoline. The causes for such lynchings were reported as murder, theft, back talking, and assault--but the common thread to both the early stereotype of the "black brute" and the number of lynchings that skyrocketed around the turn of the century *was the rape of white women*:

> The frequency of these lynchings calls attention to the frequency of the crimes which causes lynching. The "Southern barbarism" which deserves the serious attention of all people North and South, is the barbarism which preys upon weak and defenseless women.

"Attacks"--a phrase synonymous with physical/sexual assault or rape--could also merely consist of whistling at, eyeballing, or simply being alone with white women. Sometimes the cry of rape was merely a mask for something else. Frequently, white women feared that their being alone or having any contact with a black male would smear their reputation, and as recourse--only an inference that something improper had happened was required, with little care for what ensued thereafter. Hysteria played a huge part in the erosion of law and order which culminated in mass lynchings. Innocence or guilt rarely mattered. In light of this, I was anxious to see what had been the cause for the lynching at Valley Park, which may well have been any of these.

The St. Louis area had been the scene of another horrible tragedy many years before the lynching in Valley Park. A free man, Francis McIntosh, was lynched on the outskirts of St. Louis on the 28th of April, 1836. Accused of "Murder and Murderous Assault of Law Officers", he was chained to a tree and burned alive. A witness wrote:

> After the flames had surrounded their prey, and when his clothes were in a blaze all over him, his eyes burnt out of his head, and his mouth seemingly parched to a cinder, someone in the crowd more compassionate than the rest, proposed to put an end to his misery by shooting him, when it was replied, that it would be of no use, since he was already out of his pain. "No," said the wretch, "I am not, I am suffering as much as ever,-shoot me, shoot me." "No," said one of the fiends, who was standing about the sacrifice they were roasting, "He shall not be shot; I would sooner slacken the fire, if that would increase his misery," and the man who said this was, we understand, *an officer of justice*.

When this case was before the Grand Jury, Judge Luke Lawless (some might say aptly named) spoke the following:

> "If... the destruction (of McIntosh) was the act as I have said, of the *many*--of the multitude, in the ordinary sense of those words--not the act of numerable and ascertainable malefactors, but of congregated thousands, seized upon and impelled by that mysterious, metaphysical, and almost electric frenzy, which, in all nations and ages, has hurried on the infuriated multitude to deeds of death and destruction--then, I say, act not at all in the matter--the case then *transcends* your jurisdiction--it is beyond the reach of human law."

The lynching was nationally reported at the time, and remarked upon by such notable men as Abraham Lincoln, and the Abolitionist Rev. Elijah P. Lovejoy. The lynching of McIntosh summoned the disgust and rhetoric of the local St. Louis editor Lovejoy--and consequently led to his own death a year later--by an angry mob on the Mississippi River. Lovejoy's death was observed as a turning point in the abolitionist cause. A notable white man had been killed for his views against slavery. Stirred by Lovejoy's assassination, a young John Brown is said to have thenceforward dedicated his life to the destruction of slavery.

It is important to remember that later St. Louis would continue to have a tormented racial situation; in the north-side race riot in Fairgrounds Park in 1949, but perhaps most notably--in the East St. Louis race riot of 1917.

On May 28th, 1917, while at a city meeting-

-the Mayor of East St. Louis and other city officials blasted the recent importation of southern blacks to the area for labor purposes, and a small riot ensued afterwards. Throughout the following month, resentment and hostilities quietly grew between the white and black citizens of East St. Louis.

On the night of Sunday, July 1st, an armed group of blacks killed Detective Sergeant Samuel Coppedge, and wounded three other officers. Four companies of the 4th Regiment of the Illinois National Guard were dispatched, and marched into the streets of East St. Louis with fixed bayonets. Black passengers were pulled from streetcars and beaten or stoned to death. Storeowners were shot by stray bullets; ordinary black residents were hunted down by angry whites in their own front yards.

The St. Louis Daily Globe-Democrat reported that white women hurled bricks at black women as they fled there homes, and cited a gruesome detail, "I saw a member of the riot cleave a negro's head open with a hatchet." The Tuesday edition of the Globe-Democrat ran with the headline, "MAN-HUNTING MOBS BURN 60 HOMES AND SLAY FLEEING BLACKS BY BULLET AND ROPE."

More than a hundred black citizens had been killed, and it would not cease for days. The culture of racial violence--which picked up momentum in the early decades of the twentieth century--only heightened agitation between white men, black men, and officers of the law everywhere in the United States. Integration, the influx of blacks into the north, and competition for jobs only widened the divide that had existed since slavery. Despite laws that attempted to level rights and protection for all people, regional conflicts continued, sometimes ending with federalized troops--sometimes ending with the death of innocents.

Other racial incidents were caused not only by race hatred, but also in response to violent *crime*. In Sikeston, Missouri on January 20, 1942, a black mill worker named Cleo Wright assaulted a white woman in her home, and then stabbed a police officer in the neck when fleeing the scene. Later that day, Wright was taken from the Sikeston jail by a mob, chained to a car bumper--and dragged through the streets of Sunset Addition--the black district of Sikeston. He was then taken to a stretch of train tracks, and burned alive with a gallon of gasoline and a lit match.

These past moments in time are shameful reminders of another world which our nation would love to soon forget from its collective soul. Nevertheless, they play a role in painting an accurate picture of our world as it once was. Valley Park, St. Louis, or for that matter the state of Missouri is far from Salem, Massachusetts--and that of their famous witch trials of centuries ago--yet, as we can see, we Missourians were not always that far removed.

Though we choose to be selective in our commemorations of things past, there are still some things that haunt us. We have come to know the stories of our racial past, and have grown to reluctantly accept them. But then, there *is* one that we still have yet come to know; we have what happened in Valley Park--outside of the problems of the city-- out in the peaceful farms and mills of St. Louis County. It is not a secret that should be kept.

Most residents never know of the history that has transpired in their very own town, on their very own playground. Perhaps all playgrounds have a story of tragedy that haunts them. Who knows just how many stories die with the closed lips of a forgotten generation. Assuredly, *Valley Park is mature enough to have many.*

In 1894, according to state records, two lynchings occurred in the state of Missouri; one in Callaway County, and one in St. Louis County. The record states that on January 17, 1894, John Buckner--a black citizen of Valley Park--was charged with "criminal assault and attempted criminal assault," and was lynched for the crime. The state record fails to record the mythic tale of this man's demise, simply labeling the death as "private."

I checked into some resources on the web, and found nothing. I checked libraries, bookstores, and found no bearing on the subject. What I did manage to find was usually lost in a compilation of unrelated stories or in undistributed local narratives, and only hinted at what happened. Only the same snippet of information, again and again: "John Buckner, January 17, 1894, Valley Park, MO. Private." Valley Park itself had no record, public or private, of a lynching. If indeed there was a lynching--*there seemed to have been no investigation conducted by the authorities.* The state records seemed to have nothing on the subject. There were no accusers, no witnesses who came forth, and no attempt by the state at finding the lynch mob. It was as if he had committed suicide.

I did find this, however. The very next afternoon after Buckner had been lynched; the coroner had cut down the body and wrote out the verdict on the spot for the County authorities:

> We, the jury, find that John Buckner came to his death at the hands of a person or persons unknown to the jury.

These words should be all too familiar to anyone familiar with the language of lynching. It is the "*cliché*" of this subject. Reading a verdict like the one above, one can almost picture a devilish smirk on the law officer's face as he wrote it out. Those who lynched this man were probably part of the "jury." Lynching was--99 times out of 100--a crime which went unpunished. In the very few cases that have been prosecuted, even fewer have been convicted. These "unknown" persons who lynched--never reveal to us guilt or innocence, motive, reason, or name. Looking at what little I had found, I wondered if anyone *really did* want to know who had lynched this man, John Buckner. As a later article said, "The people want no inquiry. The matter ended with the verdict of the Coroner's jury." End of story.

I had run into a wall. Perhaps there would be nothing left about this incident to find. Other than the collections of the Missouri Historical Society and the archival microfilm of local newspapers, little else was recorded, and little has survived thus far. It has been over 100 years since this incident happened. No local historians ever put down their recollections for us to find. Also, as one elder resident told me--some things were simply "not talked about" openly in earlier times.

I decided to make a trip to the microfilm archive of the St. Louis Main Public Library, where I knew that the records of numerous St. Louis daily newspapers were kept in rolls in the basement. Perhaps, if the story had been covered in the St. Louis papers--I might find some corroboration and much needed insight to this incident--and into the *St. Louis* of January 1894.

January 1894

On the morning of Friday, January 12, 1894, a white convict named Sam Welsor was to be hanged at the St. Louis City Jail, known as the "four courts," for the murder of his mistress. In the early hours of August 4, 1890, Sam Welsor had gone to the home of his estranged lover Donizabel Clementine Manning, who had recently won $5,000 dollars in a lottery drawing. When she refused to split the amount with him, Welsor seized her by the hair, threw her to the floor, and with a foot on her chest—fired five bullets into her helpless body.

This would be a *state* execution, witnessed by local personalities, politicians, and a tightly packed, rowdy mob of spectators. Crowds had begun to assemble hours before and grew to such a number that officials realized they no longer held possession of the jail. Whiskey bottles were passed around the press of the hundreds of people trying to shove their way in to witness "the death of the unfortunate criminal." It was speculated that tickets to the event cost anywhere from six to fifteen dollars. At the last minute a few VIP guests were also ushered in by the top St. Louis officers, at no charge. The <u>St. Louis Star-Sayings</u> commented on the disgraceful scene:

> Not until the corridor of the Four Courts was frightfully packed did the police realize that it was about time to do something. It was then too late, however. Not a blue coat could get into the tightly wedged mass of humanity, and every effort they made to thin the crowd and establish the semblance of order was greeted with yells of derision and jeering remarks.

A rumble of voices and applause preceded the escort of officers who marched into the courtyard with Sam Welsor. It was noted that the condemned man marched with "a firm step" as he walked past the crowds towards the scaffold. A reporter present at the execution wrote the following:

> Welsor never faltered as he reached the stairway leading up to the trap, and when he had gained the platform, turned around and surveyed the immense crowd below with a calm expression. A half-smile passed across his face for an instant, as he asked the Sheriff to remove his hat for him, saying, "I can't do it myself. I'm handicapped by these," indicating the ropes which bound his arms. A small box was placed in the center of the trap door and this Welsor mounted, while a Deputy Sheriff pinioned his legs. Just before the black cap was placed over his head, Welsor was asked by Sheriff White whether he wished to say anything. "No," he replied, determinedly, "Go ahead."

The crowd moved back, and by a silent signal, the

trap was sprung. After hanging for a full fifteen minutes, the body was cut down. The Star-Sayings wrote, "The crowd in the jail yard made a mad rush for the scaffold, in their mad eagerness to obtain a piece of the rope which had been used in the execution, in accordance with a superstition current among certain classes that the possession of such a ghastly souvenir portends good luck and success to the fortunate possessor of life."

Sam Welsor's hanging had gone forward an hour late, but with "no problems thereafter." The crowd filtered into neighboring bars, discussing the spectacle they had just witnessed. It was universally admitted that the doomed man had "died game." The local media, however, characterized the chaotic scene as an embarrassment to the entire city. It was roundly denounced by both long-standing opponents to the death penalty and by those who merely abhorred the spectacle of a publicly viewed execution. Critics saw the death of even the most fiendish criminal as a solemn and "private" affair, not to be an event for spectators. Others felt strongly that public punishment for crime was essential as a viable deterrent. For the next few days, politicians, police, and concerned citizens became polarized over the issue, until they were distracted by other events.

In 1894, the execution of those who committed murder, rape, and theft was usually carried out by hanging. Almost each week's newspaper contained a half dozen articles about a hanging going on in some manner--either by the state or "Judge Lynch"--all across the United States. Until the early 1890s this form of execution was the primary form of capital punishment, until legislators sought to find a more humane way of punishing condemned criminals. Their solution was an invention made through the collaboration of an inventor named Harold Brown, and another named Thomas Edison. On August 6, 1890 at Auburn Prison in New York, William Kemmler, a man who had "chopped a woman to bits with an axe"-- became the first man to die in the electric chair. The maiden run was far from a success; after an initial attempt, the condemned man was found to be still painfully alive, and after a gruesome second try, the man's body caught on fire. Primarily as a result of the electric chair's botched first try, hangings continued across the country.

By the time of Welsor's execution in 1894, the crimes for which men were often hanged rapidly began to touch the people of the St. Louis area. Since 1876, the city had been legally separate from the County. Crime had always been a factor in urban areas; now in 1894--it had spread to the rural farms well outside of the city. In the previous months, St. Louis County had become the place of several robberies, assaults, and unprovoked murders; at homes of prominent citizens, and on the county roads that had now become unsafe to travel alone.

On May 20th, 1893, north St. Louis County was aroused by the killing of Ben McColloch, a bank teller who lived near Ferguson, found dead on the porch of his residence. An empty shotgun and revolver were found near his body, which had been hit with a load of buckshot:

It appeared evident that Mr. McColloch had been awakened by burglars and that, armed with the shotgun, he had gone out on the porch to meet them. There was a struggle, which ended in the banker being shot with his own weapon.

Later that September, Edgar Fitzwilliam, a motorman for the Midland Electric Road, was murdered by four black assailants who held him up in his car "...pulled the trolley of the wire, plunging the car into total darkness..." and then shot him.

Charles Williams, a black resident of the county, leaked to police that two brothers--James and Edward Murray, both black men, had murdered Fitzwilliam. This lead had come as Charles Williams was himself a prisoner, under arrest for larceny. Once the St. Louis Police had arrested Jim Murray for the murder, he in turn made incriminating statements about a William Hensley, who was then picked up as an accessory. Then, early in January, while still incarcerated in the Clayton Jail, Ed and Jim Murray swore out an affidavit that both Williams and Hensley were the unknown suspects in the Ben McColloch slaying the year before.

The complicated history of African-Americans is often intertwined with the history and implementation of American Justice. 1894 was no different. African-American men were in the late nineteenth century just as equally *subjected* to violence and crime—if not more so--than they themselves may have been accused *or actually guilty of.* In many instances--an unsolved crime, a missing object, a lack of sufficient employment—or simply any situation that lacked explanation, a black man at most times would be counted as among the prime suspects.

In Black Rock, Arkansas, on the morning of January 6th, citizens awoke to find dozens of notices posted all along their streets that warned all "negroes" to leave town, and that white property owners who did not have their black occupants vacate would have their property *burned to the ground*. There were three to five hundred blacks in Black Rock, and the mill owners had been employing many of them instead of local white labor to operate their mills. "Several barns have been burned in portions of this county," reported one newspaper, "and it looks as if a vigilance committee would have to get to work."

At about 1 o'clock on the same morning, a 16-year-old boy, Roscoe Parker, was taken from an Ohio jail and lynched by an armed and masked mob. He had been accused of murdering an aged couple, by bludgeoning then with a heavy club and cutting their throats with a butcher knife. The newspaper reported that "the negro lad" had been lynched without joy, but added, "…it was richly deserved."

Meanwhile, in the city and county of St. Louis, events escalated. In the early hours of January 13th, a St. Louis night watchman named W. E. Craig discovered a blood soaked hat, lying on the sidewalk. A trail of blood stretched across the street to the opposite curb; "Enough blood, " one witness said, "to kill *any* man." The mysterious crime scene was near the corner of Morgan Street and Taylor

Avenue, in the city's West End. Doctor's confirmed that the blood was human, and the Police soon discovered additional drops of blood in the vacant lots adjacent to the street. A night watchman at a local livery stable recalled that an hour or so before, he had heard the loud noises of a wagon and angry voices rush past, one of the men saying, *"My God, Don't kill me!"* Officers developed the theory that a murder had indeed taken place, and then been transported from the scene in a spring wagon, though there was, as of yet, no body found of "…the unfortunate man, whoever he is, from whom flowed the quart or more of blood which stains the pavement."

Then, in the early evening hours of January 16th, a farmer, Thomas Fitzgerald, and a companion, C. S. Link, were riding back from the city along the St. Charles Rock Road in St. Louis County. Far ahead along the road a wagon had stopped, and three men had jumped out and started walking back towards them. As they came upon the wagon, one of the men suddenly seized Fitzgerald's horses, as another pulled out and leveled a revolver. The third man began searching the two victims. When it was realized that the farmer Fitzgerald had no money--the armed man shot Fitzgerald point blank in the chest.. Fitzgerald's companion Link pleaded with them to stop, and was grazed by a second bullet. Link then was searched, and relieved of all the money he had. Fitzgerald soon died. The murderers had been three black men:

This is the fifth of a series of highway robberies in that neighborhood since Friday. All of them were perpetrated by Negroes. These, with the recent murders committed in St. Louis County, have aroused the farmers to a state of desperation and determination to make an example of the criminals if caught.

So far in the new year, violent crime had become the primary threat to the farmers, merchant's and settlers out in the County of St. Louis. Basically out in the wilderness, the law was enforced only as soon as the nearest Peace officer could arrive on horseback from the County seat in Clayton, a good hour's ride from most of the homes in Bonhomme Township. This was of course only after a victim of crime had to first make a ride *simply to report it to authorities*--in person. There was no 911 emergency; there were no patrol cars minutes away; nor were there any local police departments. Any semblance of Justice often relied on good neighbors, a good rifle, and depended on speed.

Due to delayed and insufficient law and order, many people suffered at the hands of criminals unchecked by the law or repeat offenders--already "rehabilitated" by the state. As a result, many citizens felt that the system was not adequate to handle the needs of the law-abiding people of the community. One man wrote:

The presence and pernicious activity of criminals in the county are the effects of a plain cause. Criminals naturally seek the safest place to commit crime. They go where there is the least danger of arrest and punishment. When a locality is infested with thugs, it is safe to conclude that the laws are not enforced with efficient vigor.

After months of terror, an overwhelming feeling of frustration and desperation was fostered among the law-abiding citizens of St. Louis County. The execution of Sam Welsor earlier that week had wildly excited the area. To many officers of the law, it seemed that the pent up feelings of the victimized populace were at last at a boiling point. His execution, the lynching of Roscoe Parker in Ohio, and the triple lynching of three self-confessed murderers by a Kansas mob on January 14--led Captain Boyd, of the Saint Louis Police to remark:

> I think... that a public execution, when conducted properly, where the gallows is erected in a place which can be seen by all, say in a great field or vacant lot, is the most powerful lesson that can be taught on the effects of crime. A young man or woman, or an older person, who has seen a hanging will never forget it... If the hanging cannot be perfectly public it should be absolutely *private*.

A writer for the <u>Evening Star-Sayings</u> wrote the following:

> The law which condemns (a criminal) to death was not enacted solely for the purpose of removing from this world a man who has proved himself a menace to his fellow men, but was placed upon the statute books in order that an example might be made which should, if possible, prevent others from committing a similar crime. Its execution should be carried out with all the solemnity due to the enforcement of the most extreme penalty of the law.

By the afternoon of Wednesday, January 16th, 1894, as the death of the farmer Fitzgerald was announced, with no prospects for the apprehension of his murderers--a disquieted furor consumed the people of St. Louis County. One officer of St. Louis County would later recall that around that time, "he had been expecting something to happen."

THE SCENE OF THE HANGING.

St. Louis Main Public Library

The Lynching

On the night of Tuesday, January 16th, 1894, the presses of the <u>St. Louis Republic</u> newspaper printed the headline for the next morning's paper:

THIS CALLS FOR HEMP

St. Louis County the Scene of a Shocking Outrage.--
A Negro's Double Crime.--
...The Brute Captured and in a Fair Way to Be
Summarily Dealt With.

The newspaper and telegraph offices were buzzing that evening about a story that had citizens all over St. Louis and St. Louis County infuriated and indignant. Delia Mungo, "...a rather comely colored lady of 33 years of age," and Miss Althea Harrison, the 19-year-old white daughter of a prominent farmer, had both been sexually assaulted in Valley Park that afternoon. A young local black man, known to both of the victims, was quickly named as the culprit. Almost immediately, people on the city streets; farmers and merchants riding the county roads; passengers riding the trains between Valley Park and St. Louis--soon spread the news of what had happened. Within hours, hundreds of normally peaceful county residents from Manchester, Fenton, Valley Park, and the county seat of Clayton--would load their weapons and set off on their horses for the scene of the crime. That evening, the Republic would make the prediction that "...should a mob be organized at Valley Park and come here before this mob disperses, the chances are that the Coroner will have a job by daylight."

By the afternoon of the next day, the St. Louis Globe-Democrat's headline was simply, *"SETTLED BY JUDGE LYNCH."* "The body of John Buckner, a negro ravisher," so said the January 17th edition of the St. Louis Post-Dispatch, "hung suspended at a rope's end beneath the span of the county bridge over the Meramec River at daybreak, this morning." The St. Louis Star-Sayings led with, *"BUCKNER LYNCHED.--Enraged Citizens of St. Louis County Make Short Work of a Colored Fiend."* Readers of the St. Louis newspapers awoke that morning to a full account of the night's events, complete with detailed drawings of the lynching-- one of which documented the crowds of onlookers, gawking from the riverbank at the hanged man.

The victim of the lynching was a grandson to one of the earliest free black settlers in St. Louis County, from which he took his name. The Buckner family was comprised of the eight children of John and Vinette Buckner, who had moved to St. Louis from Kentucky in the mid-nineteenth century: the youngest--Freeman, age 31, named after the

Emancipation Proclamation of 1863, then Joseph, James, Sarah, Lewis, Mary, John, and William, age 47--the oldest, and father of one girl and four boys-- Eliza, James, Harry, Elisha, and John Buckner, age 23. Their neighbors were Albert and Delia Mungo, a black couple who also had roots in St. Louis County. A farmer and a laundress, they owned their own land, and had a reputation for being refined, "...intelligent and respectable."

They lived in a hilly area just south of the Meramec River, along the Hawkins Road; a mere three miles south of the town of Valley Park. The Buckner men were laborers and farmers, as were most other black men in the area. John Buckner's uncle John owned five acres of land next door to the Mungo family. We know little else. As is the case with so many African-American ancestors--there are no birth records; no death certificates; no photographs.

The first record we have of John Buckner is that which is on the 1880 Federal Census, when he was age 9. The next is his indictment for "assault with intent to rape," on November 21, 1889--when he was only 17 years old. The victim was Mrs. Mary V. Weaver, a "colored" schoolteacher in Valley Park. Buckner pleaded not guilty, and a trial was set for the St. Louis County Circuit Court in Clayton. On December 5th, Judge Edwards heard the case:

> Almost the whole day on Thursday and up until a late hour Thursday night Judge Edwards was engaged in hearing evidence in the case of State vs. John Buckner... A large

number of witnesses attested to the excellent
character of the prosecuting witness. The
defendant was represented by Zach J. Mitchell
and George W. Royse. The case was resumed
yesterday morning, when the arguments were
made and the case given to the jury at 11 o'clock
a.m. After remaining out six hours the jury
returned a verdict of guilty and assessed his
punishment at three years in the Penitentiary.

On December 10, 1889, John Buckner arrived in
Jefferson City, Missouri and was registered as
prisoner number 8392 at the Missouri State
Penitentiary:

> Name: John Buckner
> Age: 17
> Nativity: Missouri
> Trade: Farmer
> Height: 5 ft 10-1/4 in
> Length Foot: 10-3/4
> Hair: Blk
> Eyes: Blk
> Complexion: Copper
> Marks and Scars: Single-Parents
> Meramec St. Louis County Mo.
> Short flat nose, Scar in left eyebrow,
> Vaccin scar Muscle left arm.
> Weight: 185 lbs.

Even at age 17, Buckner was no small man. At the
time, anything over 5'7" was considered "tall."
Most schoolchildren have been taught to imagine
the mythical president Abraham Lincoln as a
towering giant--but, in his stocking feet at 6'4"--by
today's standards, Lincoln would have been
surpassed by a large amount of men, as would have
Buckner. In 1894 however, Americans were

typically shorter. Unlike today, an ordinary person's diet in the nineteenth century kept most people slim to slightly anorexic. At nearly six-foot- -and just under 200 lbs, John Buckner would have been considered a large man.

John Buckner was sentenced to three years from December 10, 1889--but was released just after three-fourths time, on March 10, 1892. From all accounts, he returned to the area, obtaining a residence in the city of St. Louis. "St. Louis had been his residence," reported the St. Louis Republic in January 1894, "and odd jobs around the city furnished his livelihood. Two weeks ago, however, he returned to his father's house and spent his time loafing about the neighborhood. He did nothing other than hunt and hang about the Valley Park alehouses."

In the early hours of January 18th, 1894, a Frisco Railroad employee, Fireman T. J. Watson, was interviewed by the St. Louis Star-Sayings:

> I saw John Buckner, the miscreant, ...near Valley Park yesterday afternoon,...but he wasn't very lively. He was hanging to the stringers of the first span of the bridge on the road between Manchester and Valley Park. That was where the lynching party left him when they had no further use for him. ...They said the crowd was wild, and nothing would satisfy them but the miscreant's life. The victim was stubborn and defiant at first, then pleaded innocence and begged for mercy, but after his identification by Mrs. Mingo (sic) there seemed to be but one wish of the assembled mob, and the mad howl went up, lynch him, lynch him.

William O. Pratt was a brakeman on the Frisco
accomidation train:

> When the train reached St. Louis I was
> informed that the negro had been caught and had
> been lynched, on what is known as the county
> bridge, which bridge is situated between the
> Missouri Pacific and Frisco Railroad tracks, and
> about three blocks from the former road station.
> When I returned to Valley Park, which was at 9
> o'clock I saw the negro hanging from the side of
> the bridge. He wore dark clothes and was
> hatless. His hands were handcuffed together in
> front of him, while his feet had been securely
> tied with a strong piece of rope. The rope used
> in launching the negro into eternity was, I should
> judge, over an inch in thickness. The fall the
> ravisher received when he met his death must
> have been over ten feet. Large crowds of people
> were standing on the ground and bridge viewing
> the remains as it was dangling from the rope.
> No one, it appears, made any attempt to cut the
> body down, and at noon, when I left Valley
> Park, the body was still hanging.

About the lynching, one man had written, "Nobody
knew who had done the deed and nobody cared to
know. All they knew was that justice had been
meted out." The St. Louis Republic described in
detail the crimes of the 16th, that had sent St. Louis
County into a frenzied manhunt, and sealed
Buckner's horrific end:

> About 2 o'clock that afternoon he took a
> shotgun belonging to his father, presumably to
> hunt, and strolled towards Valley Park along the
> Hawkins Road. On his way he passed the cabin

of Mrs. Mungo, but she was not in. Continuing along the road he came to the identical spot where he had assaulted Miss Weaver. Here he met Mrs. Mungo.

The Post-Dispatch continues from there:

> She knew he was an ex-convict,... and so divining his purpose asked him kindly to let her pass. He refused and made an insulting proposal. Then she begged piteously to be allowed to go home to her sick baby, promising not to say anything about his actions if he would not detain her. Instead of granting her request, however, he knocked her down with the butt of his gun, dragged her into some timber nearby and accomplished his foul purpose.
>
> Leaving her in the timber bruised, bleeding and almost unconscious, he continued his walk to the Harrison home. On carefully looking about the place, he discovered that Mr. Harrison's beautiful 19-year-old-daughter Alice was at home alone. He did not force his way into the house, but patiently waited until the unsuspecting girl went into one of the outbuildings. Then he pounced upon her, tearing off the lock on the door of the building wherein she was to gain admission. When he seized her a terrible struggle ensued. The poor, timid girl nerved with the strength of desperation fought fiercely, savagely for her honor, while the black fiend, thoroughly enraged at this unexpected resistance, scratched and pounded her almost into insensibility, all the time threatening to kill her if she did not give in.

According to the St. Louis Globe-Democrat, the young girl injured Buckner as he tried to force himself on her:

To stop her cries for assistance, the brute placed his hand over her mouth, when, quick as thought, she closed her teeth upon one of his fingers. This turned the tide of battle, and Buckner, actually yelling with pain, beat her beautiful features almost into a jelly in his efforts to release his imprisoned finger. The struggle must have lasted fully ten minutes, when from sheer exhaustion the brute relaxed his bind upon the young lady, and she escaped to the house of a neighbor, Mr. James Vandover, where she was sheltered until the arrival of her father.

After Mrs. Mungo had learned the common fate of young Allie Harrison, she ran down the Vandover Road and informed her husband of what had been done. Albert Mungo sent her into the house, and got on his horse. The family members of both victims promptly set out for the only lawman in the area--the constable who held reign over the Bonhomme township, and the entire southwest region of St. Louis County. Along the way, both Mr. Harrison and Mr. Mungo alerted those they passed of the earlier assaults of Buckner. At the city of Manchester, a few miles northwest of Valley Park--the Constable, Nicholas Schumacher, was found. As small groups of farmers, storekeepers, and landowners standing outside of his office learned of the double assault, Schumacher wrote out the warrant for John Buckner. He then got in his buggy and headed towards Valley Park.

Angry county residents were meanwhile searching the woods all around the Meramec River for the familiar form of John Buckner. Hurriedly passing them in his buggy on the Quinette Road was Dr. John A. Gandy from nearby Barrett's Station, enroute the homes of the battered victims Mrs. Mungo and Miss Harrison. "Persons who saw (Allie Harrison's) room after the struggle," said the Star-Sayings, "declare that it looked like a slaughter-house. Blood, bits of clothing and tufts of the poor girl's hair were all over the room." Mrs. Mungo was said to be inconsolable. Gandy would later report that their physical wounds would fully heal. As to their emotional and mental state after their experience, he said: "they may never *fully* recover." As the sun began to set, more and more people were seen scouring the streets and woods between Manchester and Valley Park, all along the Marshall and Quinette roads for the accused.

In the face of a potentially volatile situation, the few lawmen of St. Louis County grew apprehensive that their suspect might have already eluded capture and fled. The Constable however was not concerned. Schumacher later recollected his feeling to a descendant—that he knew that *he alone* would find Buckner. Despite the common misconception that a great majority of criminals run and hide--in his experiences with criminal behavior, Schumacher had learned that the first places a criminal will visit after committing a crime and escaping unharmed is the home of a family member, friend, or simply return to their own. Thus, Schumacher in his search bypassed the scene of the crime and Valley Park, and instead headed south--across the old wagon bridge to where he had a hunch Buckner would be.

By this time, several people had

accompanied and or trailed the Constable enroute his destination. At around six o'clock, Constable Schumacher arrived at the suspect's home-- a cabin which was soon surrounded from all sides. He knocked at the front entrance and waited. The door opened, and at once, he entered. He encountered Buckner's family seated in the front room. Walking back into an interior room, pistol in hand— Schumacher slowly opened a door. There, seated at a table sat John Buckner--coolly smoking an old corncob pipe. "I want you," said Schumacher. Upon recognizing the Constable, Buckner rose up, and dashed for his father's shotgun--hanging opposite him on the wall. Before he could, Schumacher leveled his pistol at Buckner, again saying, "You're wanted *you sonofa'bitch*." At the sound of the click from Schumacher's pistol-- Buckner froze in place, halfway to the wall where his weapon hung. Handcuffs were placed on Buckner, and he was taken outside to the Constable's wagon. In the meantime, members of the two victim's families and other angry citizens of St. Louis County had gathered; determined to take Buckner themselves, many of them shouting, "String 'em! String 'em!" Assessing the situation, Constable Schumacher quickly mounted, and hastily rode off with the prisoner:

> It was moonlight, ever so clear and beautiful. The rough roadway was lighted up with the peaceful glimmer and sheen, making the faces of the captive and guardsman perfectly visible. The three and a half miles to Valley Park were soon traversed, over the same wagon bridge, the identical iron beam from which a few hours later the prisoner was to swing lifeless. Across the bridge in the village they found

56

citizens awake and stirring. The news had brought many out and gathered them about the taverns. While passing, some of the guard dropped back. They mingled with the crowd and gave the particulars of the arrest. A few moments more and someone from the crowd cried:

"Hev you got him?"

"Yes," called back Schumacher.

"Hold on, then," came the command, to which the constable answered by whipping his horse and leaving the crowd some distance behind. The crowd was not to be robbed of its prey so easily, however.

A reporter from the St. Louis Republic had caught a train out to Valley Park and had arrived there just in time to see the procession come past across the bridge into town. He ran up and asked Buckner if he was indeed guilty of the crimes he had been charged with. "The negro acknowledged to your reporter that he had accomplished his purpose with Mrs. Mungo," said the reporter, "but will not talk about Miss Harrison." As the reporter wrote down Buckner's statement, constable Schumacher stepped down to speak with someone along the road. Within moments, from the center of town came a sudden rush of numerous men intent on taking custody of the prisoner, and once again the shouts came, "String him!"

Nicholas Schumacher and the suspect Buckner now hastily left Valley Park for the city of Manchester, a forty-five minute ride. Once beyond the homes of Valley Park, Schumacher could see little in front or behind of them. It was now dark, and every shadowy shape on the horizon presented a precarious situation. Several times, as they traversed the Meramec Station Road, they were startled by the sight or sound of men in pursuit on horseback. Each time, the constable sped up and lost his pursuers. Looming in the rear, however-- one clandestine horseman followed the constable's wagon, at a considerable distance. Nor did they know what awaited them up ahead. Once they had reached Manchester, Schumacher took Buckner before Squire Frank Hofstetter, who committed him to the Clayton Jail under $1,000 dollar bond. As the legal papers were drawn up, several in the room questioned Buckner:

> At first he denied any knowledge of the assault, but his answers, impelled by fright, entrapped him.
> "You were out hunting," said one. "Did you catch any game?"
> "No sir," answered Buckner.
> "Then where did you get this blood on your clothes? Did it come from Mrs. Mungo or Miss Harrison?"
> "I didn't do anything to Miss Harrison," was Buckner's reply. The questioners smiled and jested over the answer and accused the villian in fierce language of his crimes. He only blanched and stammered but said little more.

The options were not good. Nicholas Schumacher knew that he needed to transfer John Buckner to the County Jail as soon as possible. It was late, and the temperature outside had dropped. He could not yet safely traverse the roads to Clayton with his prisoner. Neither could he keep his prisoner where he presently was. Confronted with a potential lynching or other organized mob violence, Schumacher made a potentially fateful decision--to hide Buckner in the cellar of Justice Hofstetter's house on 2nd Street, right there in Manchester until morning. He quickly deputized the two men nearest him; John Seibert and Justice Hofstetter. "He had not misjudged the situation," said The Republic, "for ten minutes after he had passed through Valley Park with his prisoner the news had spread in every direction that the negro had been captured and was on his way to Manchester." At least twenty five to thirty men, armed with shotguns, rifles, and carbines mounted on fleet horses, and started up the road to Manchester. Meanwhile, three miles to the south in Valley Park, at least 150 citizens of Valley Park formed in a body in front of the post office to discuss what had happened. By the end of the meeting, a large group of men were quietly planning, as a few people had already decided to let the law take it's course, and went home to bed. By ten o'clock, the streets of Valley Park were deserted. Behind a few lit windows, men stood around and discussed "...what ought to be done."

The St. Louis Post-Dispatch describes in detail what happened next:

> At midnight the crowd had dispersed and not a soul was in sight. Two hours later, a light appeared in one of the saloons. It was the signal and a few minutes later a few horsemen reined in front. Nobody asked any questions and the subject of lynching was not mentioned. Three quarters of an hour later, twenty-five men had assembled, some on mules, some on horses, and five in a spring wagon... The crowd represented about the best citizens of the

Southwest section of the county. Their leader had been selected four hours before, and the solitary horseman had told them where the brute was confined. The twenty-five men represented ten times that number, and each man knew what he had to do. The men of Valley Park did not come out to see them off, but lights in various houses showed they knew what was going to be done.

About this time John Buckner was attempting to sleep down in the corner of Judge Hofstetter's cellar. The lone horseman that had clandestinely followed Schumacher's wagon to Manchester sent back word to Valley Park that the hour had *now come*:

> The procession then started. The wagon which was to take the negro from Manchester to the scene of his crime had gone on a few minutes before and at 3:30 the crowd of horsemen were at Manchester. The house where Buckner was confined was pointed out to them and after demanding admittance from the guard who has him in charge, the crowd broke in the doors.

Hofstetter had nearly fallen asleep, when the squire noticed a rapping on the front door of his home, and looked out to see a large crowd of armed men:

> They swarmed about Hofstetter's door and several advanced, pounding upon the portals. To this Schumacher responded. When his face appeared the ringleaders shouted: "We want that nigger. Give him to us or we will break in and take him."

"No you won't," was the answer. "We are to protect him. I know you fellows, and if any attempt is made now you'll get in trouble. You'd better let up." The answer was received with jeers of derision. The crowd surged only more strongly and pounded against the rear entrance. In the shadow below Buckner lay shivering, speculating upon the momentary consequences of his crime.

After a few minutes, the noises stopped. Schumacher slowly unlocked the door and quietly peered out into the darkness. The angry crowd was gone.

After their failure, the mob slowly retreated back to the main square in town. There, they entered the nearby Peterson's Saloon. "Here the mob obtained liquor," said one eyewitness, " and braced themselves *for the deed*." Shortly thereafter, in an attempt to hide their identity from the officers in charge of Buckner, the mob assembled somewhere in town to pass out handkerchiefs and masks. Returning to the Squire's house a second time, around 4:00 am, they threatened to tear down the house, after the refusals of the two officers inside:

Three heavy oak doors had to be gone through, but these crumbled away against the force of the crowd, being torn from their hinges. When the cellar was reached the negro was found crouched in a corner. The guard protested, and was told that if he attempted to interfere he would be shot. He claimed the right to defend his prisoner, and upon attempting to make a stand against the crowd was disarmed and thrown aside.

Here, the St. Louis Republic picks up the story:

Lanterns were brought to the front, while the crowd surged downstairs into the cellar. In one corner, hugging the wall and the shadow, lay Buckner... "Here he is now; bind him will you?" urged the leader. Someone had a rope, another held the light, and within a moment the criminal's limbs were bound solidly together. They turned then and bundled him up the stairs. They fairly dragged him on his back, so great was the rough enthusiasm to have him out.

It was dark outside. The moon had sunk, and only by the dull, yellow flames of lantern bobbing numerously about could the negroes lineaments be distinguished. Those who saw him declare that the sight was such as to linger forever. His face was distorted with all the fear of a hunted beast. The eyes rolled wildly and great beads of sweat gathered on his forehead. Instead of pleading the miserable fellow began wailing more like an animal than a human being. It mattered little though, his agony. No one listened to him.

Nicholas Schumacher himself later spoke to the demeanor of the suspect; "Buckner is six feet tall and weighs 180 pounds, and as soon as the men put their hands on him he began to beat about them with his handcuffed hands. He knocked down two men and then one man leveled a shotgun on him and he threw up his hands." The St. Louis Post-Dispatch continued:

He begged piteously for mercy and

claimed that he had not accomplished his purpose on Miss Harrison, although he had on Mrs. Mungo. This failed to have any effect as several of the crowd were negroes who wanted to string him to the first tree. After the wretch's legs were bound at the knee the rope was wound twice around his neck and a knot made in it.

All had heard of this man's reputation. They knew of his past sexual assault on Mrs. Weaver a few years before. Most of them knew personally the two victims and their families. Now, *they had him.* The once quiet and organized citizens of St. Louis County now degenerated into a mass of angry voices. People began shouting and jostling the prisoner. Then someone in the crowd hushed them and called for order.

There, still in the quiet streets of Manchester, they calmly debated what course to take with the accused. Some of the angry citizens wanted to shoot Buckner on the spot. Some of the mob seemed intent on lynching Buckner to a nearby telegraph pole. The leaders of the mob dissented. Instead, he would be taken to the scene of his crimes. After throwing the bound suspect into a wagon, they mounted--and the long procession of the wagon and horsemen moved down the Meramec Station Road towards Valley Park. One witness later recalled, "No delay was had in getting there. The rough wagon road was jumbled over at a great rate, while the groans of the prisoner were mocked with the jeering purpose of his angry captors." On the way, the Meramec River Bridge was suggested as the final destination:

On the way a short parley of the leaders

was held and the plans for the hanging were agreed upon. The men changed places in the wagon, and when they met the few residents who had waited up to see the finale, they were told to stay back. The party divided and ten men were sent ahead to the front of the county bridge and five stayed behind the wagon. The wagon moved toward the center and when the second cross beam from the north side was reached it stopped.

It was now 4:30 a.m. Buckner was dragged from the sawdust of the wagon bed, and marched towards the riverbank. At the foot of the bridge, the first victim of that afternoon--Delia Mungo--was brought forward to identify the accused. All was quiet, as she struggled to compose herself. When Buckner saw her, his face turned away. Still traumatized by her assault, she summoned the courage to lift her hand and point her finger—and then broke the eerie silence with her words:

> He had previously admitted that he had assaulted her, but denied the story about Miss Harrison. Weak and tottering from her awful experience, the colored woman came to the ground. As soon as she saw Buckner he tried to hide his face from her but she immediately exclaimed, "That is he. That's the man. You know you are. *You know you are.*"

After Mrs. Mungo spoke, several stout men stepped forward, and grabbed Buckner, lifting him in the air:

> The brute was asked if he had anything to say, and for the first time realizing that the mob meant business, broke down and screamed

for help. Two of the five men who had been delegated to officiate as his executioners threw their arms around his neck and choked his cries. A third drew the coil of rope tight around his neck and bound it securely to the cross beam and the upright of the bridge. The five men then picked him up and threw him over the rail of the bridge. Ten feet of rope had been allowed for the drop, and the wretch's last scream was choked off before it was fairly uttered.

The <u>St. Louis Star-Saying's</u> described the scene, "All the time the wretch was begging for his life, but his appeals fell on deaf ears. He gave one awful cry as he was thrown over but the cry was cut short by the tightening of the rope as the body shot up with a rebound in the air." Here, the <u>Post-Dispatch</u> went on:

> The body shot down, checked up and rebounded half way back again and swung practically lifeless. The only light was that cast by a couple of railroad lanterns barrowed from Frisco and Missouri Pacific trainmen, many of whom reside at Valley Park. When the body was thrown over the bridge not a man at either end moved. After waiting five minutes the body was hauled up to see if life was extinct; a roll of the negro's eyes showed that he still lived and it was lowered again. For a quarter of an hour it hung before the mob dispersed.

The <u>St. Louis Globe-Democrat</u>, in words that are hauntingly tangible, described the final moments of John Buckner's life:

> While his voice was still ringing on the morning air some one at a preconcerted signal

gave the noose a jerk from behind that tightened the knot about his throat, and the next moment four stalwart men picked up the body of the ravisher and tossed it quickly over the railing of the bridge, and it dropped a distance of 10 feet with a thud that caused every timber and iron rod of the entire structure to vibrate.

The executioners stood in almost breathless silence for several minutes and then dispersed, each man going in a different direction. It was still dark and every one was able to get out of town without being identified.

The Frisco accommodation train, consisting of George Atwood, conductor, George Hanna, baggage master, and Adolph Meyer, brakeman-- were the first to bring the news of the lynching to St. Louis and elsewhere. "It was not quite 5 o'clock," reported the Post-Dispatch, "and the night operators of both the Frisco and Missouri Pacific sent the word along the line that the 1st lynching in St. Louis County had taken place about 5 o'clock." It was also reported that "Lynchers stood in the crowd and chattered about it and laughed."

In town, a few saloons reopened, in anticipation of those coming back and forth from the large crowd gathered at the foot of the bridge, where Buckner's body was slowly swinging. Some were outwardly proud of what they had done. Others stood in reckoned silence. In the calm resolution, one man simply nodded his head at the sight. Those who had stayed in the seclusion of their homes, watching from dimly lit windows, now came out to see. One resident brought forth a rifle, with the intention of mutilating Buckner's corpse:

Somebody suggested that they fill (the body) with lead, but this was set down upon. After it was settled the rope would not break and he was done for the crowd moved to the north side of the bridge and somebody swung a lantern down to show those in the dark that the job was over. Those that lived in Valley Park returned, and those who lived in the country surrounding returned to their homes.

It was ended. John Buckner was dead. Many had known him most of their lives. Many were neighbors, fellow farmers, and friends of the Buckner family. There was, according to the witnesses, no one who raged, or dissented, or mourned over what had been done, other than that of the dead man's own mother after she had learned of his fate. The next day, the St. Louis Globe-Democrat summed up the feelings of the mob that put an end to Buckner's life:

Nothing short of the death of this monster in human form could have appeased the wrath and indignation of the excited populace of that section of the county, both white and black, who pursued the officers for nearly ten miles for the purpose of lynching him, and when his lifeless body was discovered suspended from the middle span of the high iron wagon bridge over the Meramec River early yesterday morning, not a single voice was raised in disapproval of the act from the hundreds of peaceable and law-abiding citizens who gathered on the river bank to gaze upon the ghastly spectacle.

There was no remorse. The St. Louis Post Dispatch wrote of the lynching, "The crime for which John

Buckner paid the penalty with his life was the most deliberately fiendish outrage that has ever marred the history of St. Louis County." It went on, "Crime had been rampant in that vicinity for some time past, and the community was aroused. John Buckner's crime was the brand that set public sentiment ablaze... His executioners were 25 citizens of the county, *some of them members of his own race*." Each man and woman who had been involved had their own private reason for what they had done, which largely was kept private, never to be recorded. Nevertheless, a few felt the need to explain. In the next day's editorial column was found just one example of what those reasons were--a vivid statement from a man who might have been present at the lynching:

> I and my neighbors pay our taxes, respect the law and abhor anarchy. It has taken a series of the most brutal and dastardly crimes to work our people up to their present desperation. There are 32 criminals in our County jail, 21 of them are charged with felony. Among them are brutal murderers, who have shot down our best citizens in the sanctity of their homes, others have robbed and pillaged; two have assaulted women.
>
> We cannot travel the highways in safety or lie down at night with a sense of security for ourselves or our property. When we leave our families we do so with misgivings that our women folks will be assaulted and wronged in our absence. There was nothing spontaneous about the lynching of John Buckner. We had about concluded that the punishment prescribed by law was not a punishment in some cases, but a farce. The ignorant, brutal negroes who do

these awful deeds have no reverence for the majesty of the law or respect for it's decrees. They are shiftless and idle, and confinement in jail or the penitentiary carries with it neither disgrace nor discomfort. They are fed and clothed and housed for a period, and that is all they want in life.

What is to be done with such people? They rob us and are kept at our expense in a better way of life than those guilty of capital offenses through technicalities are often miscarriages of justice and in many cases the offence is reduced in degree and the punishment prescribed is imprisonment. The result is that the criminals of that stripe are not deterred by fear of extreme punishment from the commission of crime. Our people are as a unit about the justice of the fate meted out to Buckner. His death will have a marked effect in securing us better protection for our families, ourselves and our property.

Scene of the Hanging.
[Sketched to day by a POST-DISPATCH artist.]

70

The Aftermath

On the bright, sunlit morning of January
17th, the citizens of Valley Park awoke amidst the
gossip and the rumor that a man had been lynched
out in the streets, while they slept. The entire town
came out along the banks of the Meramec to see
Buckner's lifeless form sway in the morning breeze:

> Vast crowds visited the scene all
> morning, and viewed the ghastly corpse hanging
> in the bright sunlight. No arrests have been
> made up to 2 p.m. today, although it is possible
> that all the lynchers will soon be known.
> Buckner was 23 years old and weighed about
> 180 pounds.

Shortly before two o'clock that afternoon, the body
was slowly hoisted back up into the shadows of the
bridge, and the rope cut from around Buckner's
neck. Justice Hofstetter, acting as Deputy Coroner,
directed several townsmen to carry Buckner to his
wagon, and then took the body to a saloon in town,
where an inquest was held. The body of John

Buckner lay on the floor of the saloon, as the Coroner examined the corpse.

> "A jury of Valley Park citizens was summoned, which viewed the remains, and after taking what little testimony it was possible to obtain, rendered the following verdict: "We, the jury, find that deceased, John Buckner, came to his death by hanging at the hands of parties unknown to the jury."

The body was soon turned over to the victim's uncle John Buckner, who said that he would see it "decently buried." He took the remains south from Valley Park to his cabin, three miles down the road from the bridge:

> ...(H)ere last night the stiffened corpse lay, awaiting the interment it will receive today. Through the broken panes of a miserable log window the pale, cloud-broken moonlight cast it's sheen and shadow on the gaunt form of the dead, while near it, in a dark corner, wept the mother of the erring boy alone.

> Not more than a stone's throw from this log cabin stands the cabin of his first victim, Mrs. Al Mungo, who lay sick and suffering from the fearful wounds he inflicted upon her. Not far from the dead man's home, on the same farm, stands the residence of Mr. Harrison where, too, lay his injured daughter, suffering severely from the injuries she had received. In the distance, lighted by the pleasant moonlight, could be seen the crest of a hill, where not only the present assaults, but the previous one of Buckner on Mrs. Weaver nearly five years before were committed, and in a neighboring valley lies the

small baptist meeting-house and the cemetery where today Buckner will be interred.

The investigation was basically over before it started. Though the Sheriff of St. Louis County attempted to question witnesses, take sworn statements, and find those involved--there were few witnesses willing to come forward, and there were no leads on the key individuals directly involved in Buckner's death. No one was talking. The matter would be left to the Grand Jury of the St. Louis County Circuit Court.

In the next few days following the lynching, the formation of vigilance committees and rumored assaults of black men on white women became the focus of conversation and of the St. Louis daily newspapers. The very next day, ads were put out for the "Spanish Lake Protective Association" with a reward of $100 dollars for "every miscreant captured." By the Sunday after the lynching of Buckner, a column on the <u>St. Louis Star-Sayings'</u> front page led with:

CRIME MUST CEASE.

St. Louis County Citizens Organize
a Vigilance Committee.

It Will Mete Out Speedy Punishment
to All Criminals.

No Mercy Will Be Shown to Murderers,
Highwaymen and Footpads.

The Name of Vigilantes Will Become
a Terror to Evil Doers.

This resulted from the two attacks from John Buckner on January 16th--and another two reported attacks by another black man, 17 year old Horace Johnson, in Ballwin, Missouri--less than 5 miles away from Valley Park, and only a day after Buckner was lynched.

Johnson had been arrested for attempting to assault Mrs. G. W. Higgins, "an aged white lady" and Mrs. Anderson Davis, "an aged colored woman." The offences occurred on the Manchester Rock Road, mere miles from where Buckner's crimes were perpetrated, and avenged. The Globe-Democrat reported that after the lynching of Buckner, "...it was like *a spark in dry powder*.":

> His first victim was Mrs. Higgins, over 70 years of age...He entered Mrs. Higgins' residence during the absence of her companions, and, seeing that she was alone, made indecent proposals to her, and would have attempted an assault but the old lady's cries so frightened him that he ran off and left the place.

> Upon reaching the Manchester road he met an old colored lady by the name of Davis, wife of Anderson Davis, 54 years of age. He made the same proposals to her and attempted to seize her, but the old lady screamed for help and ran down the road... When they attempted to arrest him he made a desperate struggle to escape, and it required the efforts of four men to place him under arrest.

The officers, Louis Bante and brothers Robert and

William Schleusner, bound him hand and foot, and took off with their prisoner to report the matter in Ballwin, and then transfer the prisoner to Manchester. "For God's sake, boss! Don't hang me! I didn't do nothin'!" Johnson was heard crying, as he was brought into the Ballwin Jail. People began to come in with their eyes fixed on the prisoner.

While Horace Johnson was being processed, an observer loudly asked another man if he thought Johnson should hang. The man matter of factly answered that Johnson should say his prayers. As his office filled to overflowing with the boisterous and indignant crowd, Constable Schumacher hastily made out the papers for the commitment of the prisoner. The same bloodthirsty crowd that had accompanied the hanging of Sam Welsor and the lynching of John Buckner--had now arrived for Horace Johnson. Tears showered down Johnson's cheeks. His knees shook. It was remembered that, "...his entire frame trembled, and he begged the crowd not to hang him." The Constable was determined to maintain custody of his prisoner by any means. Several attempts were made to take the prisoner, which were only thwarted with the help of the arresting officers. Upon encountering a large lynch mob once in Manchester, Johnson was moved quickly to Clayton the evening of the 18th:

> About the time the Constable left Manchester in charge of his prisoner, the assembled residents of Valley Park, Barretts, Kirkwood, and other towns and villages along the Missouri Pacific Railroad were notified by telegraph to start in pursuit. All the roads leading north to the Manchester road were soon

filled with men on horseback and in vehicles, all making haste in an effort to head off the Constable and his prisoner. When the pursuers learned that the man wanted had passed on to Clayton, masked men were sent up and down the Manchester road to notify the men to assemble and make ready for an attack on the County Jail at Clayton.

The sense of justice that was exacted on John Buckner now escalated into bloodlust. In the course of the frustrating maneuvers that law enforcement had taken to evade the mob, division and chaos pervaded the normally "orderly and law-abiding" citizens of St. Louis County, who were now intent on lynching one or all of the prisoners in the County Jail, white *or* black:

> The self-appointed leaders gathered near Des Peres, where it was agreed to go to Clayton and hang Jim and Ed Murray and Wm. Hensley, the three negroes implicated in the murder of Edgar Fitzwilliam; Horace Johnson, the Ballwin negro; Samuel Austin, alias "Stringer," a young negro, who has confessed that he attempted to rape Misses Emma and Lizzie Baker in Webster Groves, and Albert Gassaway, a young one-legged white man of South Kirkwood, who criminally assaulted Miss Coleman on Meramec Highlands.

Meanwhile, Nick Schumacher was still on his way to Clayton with Horace Johnson in the back of his wagon. The St. Louis Post-Dispatch:

> At 7 o' clock all was quiet. The moon came up unusually bright to shine on a scene of perfect peace. For three hours it remained so.

Then the sound of horses' hoofs were heard coming along the North and South Road and soon a brown horse and buggy hove in sight and pulled up in front of the Court-house. From it Constable Nicholas Schumacher of Manchester quickly emerged with a 17-year-old darkey tightly handcuffed... When asked what the offense against him was the Constable admitted that it was another Buckner case; that the boy had insulted and attempted to assault two white women, and that if he had not brought him to Clayton quickly he would have been lynched. Then lynching rumors began to fly about. The morning story to the effect that the Murrays were to be strung up was revived. The news spread about the town like wildfire. Everybody got up. Horsemen seemed to ride in town on every road, and men in buggies came from all sides.

Once again (as with John Buckner) as Constable Schumacher attempted to move his prisoner--now Horace Johnson--to the Clayton jail, a large crowd anxious for lynching confronted him and his escorts. Schumacher carefully transferred custody of the prisoner to Sheriff Charles Garrett, who promptly placed Horace Johnson safely inside his cell at the courthouse. Outside, mobs on horseback and in wagons, made up of Kirkwood, Valley Park, Ballwin, Clayton, Manchester, and Des Peres citizens, gathered at Mike Fortin's saloon, across the street from the Courthouse. Clayton it seemed was no better than Ballwin. Encountering a large mob outside, and--upon receiving word that a gathering of 500 strong were on the Manchester Road, only minutes away, Sheriff Garrett decided to avoid another lynching--and/or riot. "Let them come," he said, shivering in the cold. "We'll be ready for them." He sent one man to retrieve his revolver, and another for his double-barreled shotgun. After securing the jail-door with a guard, he gathered Deputies Hencken and Gerhart. He had decided that they would remove "the prisoners who stood most in danger" to St. Louis for safety:

> Meanwhile the excitement increased. Men on foot and on horseback chased up and down the street in and out of Fortin's and Autenreith's and it became the general belief that the mob was on it's way and would reach Clayton pretty soon... he and Hencken went over to the jail. They rushed through the doors and Hencken exclaimed at the top of his voice: *"Murrays and that little nigger that Schumacher brought in, get out of here quick if you want to save your necks!"*

So on the night of the 18th, three negro prisoners--James Murray, Edward Murray (both imprisoned for murder), and Horace Johnson, were hurriedly whisked from their cells. They were gathered in such a hurry, one of the Murray's hadn't the time to put any pants on:

> "Can't help that," said the officer. "Come on" and the two big, murderous colored men and the little Manchester colored boy were hustled down the steps, across the spacious lawn in front of the Court-house and over to Autenreith's, where the rig was waiting.

> The picture of those three barefooted, coatless negroes, one of them without trousers, with terror stamped on all their faces, running across the grass in the bright moonlight, hand-

cuffed together and guarded by two officers made a picture never to be forgotten by those who saw it.

The ironic sense of déjà vu was not lost on the prisoners. Jim Murray, remembering what had happened to Buckner, reportedly jumped up and said to the Sheriff, "Give me a gun, Mr. Garrett, and I'll take care of myself."

As Garrett, the Murrays, and Horace Johnson evacuated the city of Clayton, the Deputy Sheriff Robert Schnecko, and a large posse of local citizens—stood guard out in the cold courtyard of the courthouse, to protect the remaining twenty-seven prisoners inside. Once on the road to St. Louis, another terrible ride began, as a messenger rode ahead to inform the Sheriff that the mob was "right on his heels:"

> The fugitives expected every moment to hear the clatter of pursuers' horse hoofs behind them on the frozen road. The eight miles to De Hodiamont were traversed in less than an hour, and the Sheriff breathed a sigh of relief as he marched his men into a Suburban electric car. At twelfth and Locust they got out and walked to the Four Courts.

The prisoners made it safely to the St. Louis Jail at 12:30 that night. The mob they had expected did not materialize.

"Saint Louis County is at last finally aroused...," so speculated the St. Louis Star-Sayings the following night. "The criminal assault upon Mrs. Mungo, the colored woman, and the attempted assault upon pretty Allie Harrison, blew the smoldering embers of public opinion into the fierce fire which was only quenched when the guilty fiend, John Buckner, swung at the end of 10 feet of good rope, from the Valley Park wagon bridge. "Now," the paper continued, "new fuel has been added to that fire."

Now, the calls for a Vigilance Committee were being heard from all sides of the county. Earlier that morning, President L. C. Nelson of the St. Louis National Bank had issued a call for citizens to assemble that Saturday night at C. W. Walton's grocery store in Normandy, and from there "adjourn" then to the local schoolhouse. By Saturday morning, advertisements in the newspapers asked citizens to attend the meeting, to, "…take steps to organize against the lawlessness prevalent in the county."

At 8 o' clock, on the evening of Saturday, January 20th, over 100 farmers, business merchants, and local officials and representatives hailing from as far as Valley Park, Clayton, and St. Ferdinand Township in Northern St. Louis County piled into the St. Ann parochial school-house on the Natural Bridge Road. In the back, a few blacks lined the rear wall of the auditorium. It was reported by the St. Louis Globe-Democrat as a meeting "of the foremost men of the county," and would "…render necessary immediate and most summary measures for the suppression of the criminal element." After the presiding official had announced the obvious object of the meeting, several of those present rose and spoke to the crowd. Pro-vigilante addresses by Col. Clay Taylor, James A. Reardon, and John

Bauer were endorsed by the crowd. Judge H. S. Smith of Carsonville, Missouri was reported to have said at the meeting, "*If one of the negro fiends criminally assaults or attempts to assault any of your women, catch him and string him up to the highest limit, in the tallest tree you can find.*" The Judge's remarks were loudly applauded.

Outspoken and the most spirited were the business leaders of the County and of Valley Park. Gerhardt H. Timmerman, president of the St. Louis Iron and Machine Works, was perhaps the largest property owner in Valley Park--and, who also just happened to own the land surrounding the north side of the Meramec River Bridge. " I always understood that Buckner was no good," said Timmermann afterwards. The esteemed L. C. Nelson, President of the St. Louis National Bank, presided over the committee, which he named "The Suburban Safety Association." When several speakers made racist comments regarding the specific punishment of "*negro brutes*"--Nelson dissented. The chairman made clear--that *race* would hold no distinction in the common goals of the people; to solve the common problem of the people, the committee would need the cooperation of *all* "good citizens of the county, white or black."

Those who were instrumental in the lynching on the 17th were never named, though the St. Louis Globe-Democrat stated the following insight:

The men who lynched the negro Buckner, and were hot in the chase after Horace Johnson, will be present and are unanimously in favor of organization for mutual protection. They are known to be among the county's best residents.

One man said of the committee, "The general feeling is that these outrages must be stopped at any cost, and they propose to carry out their determination to that effect *if every wagon and railroad bridge in St. Louis County must have it's swinging human body.*"

There were scores of lynchings in the following days, weeks, and months—all across this country. The tone and order of Nelson's "Suburban Safety Association" did not, however, extend to other parts of the state, or country. In New Orleans on January 19th, a crowd surrounded a black man's cabin to "horsewhip him." When he responded by opening fire on the crowd, they broke in the door and dragged him to a nearby tree "where his body was strung up and riddled with bullets."

On the 22nd, in Verona, Missouri, the 12 yr old daughter of Farmer John Jacques was raped, and two known black men were identified and pursued for days throughout southern Missouri. Two were arrested in Purdy, Missouri, while another reached the town of Billings, where he was shot at and hunted by parties of nightriders in the woods. Newspapers built up the excitement with such headlines as "ROPES READY... *The whole Country in arms.*" "Every man at Verona seems to either have a Winchester or a shotgun hunting for the fiend. One of the hardware stores has donated all of the cartridges free for those who wanted to hunt the negro." said the <u>Post-Dispatch</u>. "It is possible" it said, "that, in the excited state of the people, the Negroes under arrest at Purdy may be lynched before they are brought here."

Over 100 citizens searched all the way to Springfield in order to lynch the suspects with "the greatest excitement to prevail." Rumors of the two men disguised as women, rumored sightings of the "Negroes" at various localities, even a rumor that one of the men had already been burned at the stake soon proved false. In the following days, even those that had accused Horace Johnson began to recant their recollections. By the night of January 20th, as the "Vigilance Committee" was commencing in Normandy, the Post-Dispatch was preparing an article entitled, "JOHNSON IS INNOCENT." The St. Louis Globe-Democrat even went so far as to write an article under the heading "COMMITTED NO CRIME. *Horace Johnson Might Have Been Lynched When Innocent.*" It reported:

> The reported assault of Horace Johnson upon two aged women, near Ballwin Thursday night, that precipitated so much excitement throughout St. Louis County, upon close investigation proves to be a hoax... his first victim, yesterday volunteered the statement that she had not been assaulted by Johnson.

Johnson, it seemed, had been the cruel victim of a prank--that had become swept up in the aftermath of Buckner's crimes. Apparently, while drinking at Kern's Saloon during a free lunch, some men from St. Louis had "filled the boy with liquor until he was just drunk enough to play the fool" for the crowd:

...he had been dancing and cutting up all
afternoon for their amusement. When the crowd
had grown weary of his antics, in order to get rid
of him, they sent him down the road in search of
a woman whom they had told him called him
some very harsh names...

Johnson, quite drunk, left the drinking
establishment to pursue the imaginary slanderer.
The truth was revealed that, after first running into
Mrs. Higgins, he very politely excused himself and
continued down the road until he came upon Mrs.
Lucy Davis:

Thinking that Mrs. Davis was the
woman he had been told had been calling him
names he used some vile language for which she
had him arrested. The statements of the ladies to
their friends were misconstrued and immensely
exaggerated, and created intense excitement in
the community which was already very greatly
wrought up by the exciting events that led up to
the lynching of the negro, John Buckner, on
Wednesday morning.

The St. Louis Post-Dispatch spoke with Mrs.
Higgins, who explained what had occurred in
further detail:

"Now, I suppose he met Lucy Davis, the
colored woman he is accused of assaulting, and
put similar questions to her. She came along
after me. She had him arrested and the
excitement over the Valley Park affair did the
rest. But I'm certain there is nothing more in the
affair. I had a St. Louis relative call on Johnson
in jail. I shall not prosecute him. I blame the St.

Louis white men who got him intoxicated more than I do him. I think the boy has been done an injustice."

Horace Johnson was found not guilty after the acquittal made by Mrs. Higgins--a seventy-year-old white woman. "John Buckner committed rape and was lynched," stated a columnist, "Before the fury of the populace had subsided, Horace Johnson had the misfortune to get drunk." He was simply "the victim" of circumstances. "(This) is an able argument against mob law... showing what slight pretexts are sometimes used to justify horrible public outrages," as well as the hysteria and rumor that tends to excite and mislead the community-- said the St. Louis Republic. Even the "bloody hat"--that had been found in St. Louis in early January, presumably belonging to a mysterious murder victim--had now also been proven by police to have been a hoax.

In light of these circumstances, it was now incumbent that the matter of John Buckner finally be put to rest. Judge Rudolph Hirzel--and the Grand Jury of the St. Louis County Circuit Court--had the last word on the events of January 17th. Addressing the Grand Jury a week after Buckner was lynched, Hirzel said the following:

> While under the influence of a terrible excitement, lynching may never be morally justifiable, it never is so in law, and our good citizens should beware of such acts lest they become law-breakers themselves. As to the case on hand, I will say that from all accounts, the crime committed was so brutal and fiendish that the swift vengeance wreaked by an outraged

people is not to be wondered at. I shall, therefore, leave the matter to your careful consideration. While your prosecuting officer and your Sheriff have done all in their power, and your courts are willing to administer justice promptly, the law's delays--sanctioned by our statutes--have been the chief cause of lynching by an outraged people.

The Grand Jury agreed. On January 27th, 1894, the St. Louis County Grand Jury reported its findings on the inquiry into the lynching of John Buckner:

In obedience to special instructions, we examined quite a number of witnesses on the unfortunate lynching of the man Buckner, and we have not been able to secure any evidence sufficient to justify an indictment in the premises. In that connection, we may remark that the people of the neighborhood in which the affair occurred are of remarkably good repute for industry, intelligence, and obedience to the law, and furthermore, from all that we can learn, the cause of the lynching was the double crime of brutal assault and rape upon two defenseless women, white and black, proven and confessed, and that the man was lately released from the penitentiary for a similar crime. The extreme penalty he received by mob violence, *though wrong and lawless* in method, was done upon the most exciting and shocking of aggravations, and the severity of the punishment thus meted out to him was, after all, *no greater than the law allows.*"

Their words basically ended the matter, as far as the law could carry it. Never again would there be a lynching in St. Louis County. As time passed, there was still the occasional incident that put the vigilance committees out in force, scouring the woods for fugitive law-breakers. But, in a large part due to their vigilance--the excitement wore down, as did the crime, which had alerted the County citizens and had put both law-abiding citizens and criminals on notice. The colder temperatures hampered the crime wave also. On January 23rd, only four cases came before the courts of St. Louis. A Blizzard hit the area in the next few days, and St. Louis County started tending to other things. As the newspapers featured less and less crime, residents began to focus on the positive aspects of their community; they constructively went forward to support civic improvements, such as the new Bellefontaine Bridge, and the development of Forest Park near the outskirts of St. Louis city. Advertisements celebrated such causes as the "Farmer's Fund," and the "Lake Fund" for Forest Park--which would in time become the setting of the 1904 World's Fair.

By the turn of the century, Valley Park itself had grown into an industrious and booming place of business. Around 1910, a published history of the city of St. Louis predicted that Valley Park was on the edge of becoming a great city, that would one-day rival St. Louis. "Valley Park," it observed, " *has become a name to conjure by*." With it's active and beautiful river-scenes, the importation of large industry to the area, and prosperous and convenient railroad and hotel accommodations, Valley Park was well on it's way to becoming a town of huge potential.

Missouri State Archives

The Flood

As the end of the century came closer, the people of St. Louis County became more and more focused on industries rather than agriculture; on the city, rather than the country. People made fortunes on new businesses, along the Missouri and Meramec Rivers, along the Frisco and MO Pacific Railroad, and on the attractive real estate found in the towns all around St. Louis County, Valley Park among them.

Valley Park prospered, evolving into a magnet for companies, and somewhat of a popular recreational resort on the Meramec to both travelers and local residents--and children. By the turn of the century, the town was already becoming an important industrial center with the Valley Park Milling Company and Plate Glass factory, built around the time of the World's Fair. In 1901, the year "Valley Park" officially became the name of the town (named by G. H. Timmermann) the Glass Company secured 20 acres of land just east of the bridge, and spent between 2 to 5 million dollars to build not only the factory, but also office space, rental dwellings for it's employees, a school, a new sewer system, waterworks, and an electric light plant. It also spent $75,000 on a hotel-- completed in 1904--set high on the upper parts of town. The river-town had stood witness to a war, the Industrial Revolution, and a multitude of changes. The people of Valley Park had persevered and so had the prosperous town. But a reckoning to the town of Valley Park came nonetheless.

In the third week of August 1915, the waters of the Meramec rose to an unprecedented level, anywhere from 40 to 200 feet in the middle of town. The storms that had continued throughout the late summer had risen the banks to the upper parts of town that weekend. It was also consuming the town's main bridge that spanned over the river, and everything on both banks for miles. The August 23rd edition of the St. Louis Post-Dispatch cited that, "Hundreds of clubs, especially those on the right bank, are built close to the water, and it is believed that most of these were destroyed." It goes on to say that, "These places are usually filled to overflowing on Sundays with weekenders."

Both the Old Wagon Bridge and the Frisco Railroad Bridge were underwater, and the people were frantically trying to escape to rooftops and into the hills north of town--where only the strange sound of the roaring, angry current could be heard. Clubhouses, sheds, and small houses were seen bobbing up and down the enormous lake with frightened citizens hanging on for dear life. Three men were drowned when the shed that they were riding hit a telegraph pole. Three more died when a canoe capsized. A witness wrote:

It was awesome. The bright moonlight

added to the weirdness of the scene and assisted the little band of rescuers, which, buoyed by hope, worked nobly till daylight between Valley Park and Meramec Highlands, the main zone of danger, and up and down to Eureka and Fenton, respectively. A stream of pleasure and recreation, with a suddenness believed impossible of any unconfined waterway, turned the gayety of hundreds of club-livers and their guests into a howling, shrieking, beseeching group of frantic humans overnight.

The Post-Dispatch reported that, "Once the stream had passed the flood stage Saturday the water came down with a rush. Persons asleep in farmhouses were awakened by invading tides.... Shouts for help and the desultory firing of guns to attract rescuers could be heard for hours on both sides of the river."

That night, the massive waters of the Meramec pulled down the Old Wagon Bridge--that had stood since the time of the Civil War, from which the people of Valley Park had hung John Buckner a generation before:

By sunrise the whole section from the Frisco tracks south was submerged... The whole business part of town and most of the residence section were under water. The big steel wagon bridge below Arnold's boathouse had been swept away. The Frisco Railroad Bridge seemed to be only held in place by the two cars loaded with stone which had been run upon it for that purpose.

The river was now four miles wide at Valley Park. Witnesses on rooftops and boats were awestruck by the sound of screeching steel, and then a great moan--accompanied by the sight of the three-span steel truss bridge, vanishing beneath the angry waters of the Meramec. Farm animals, cows, debris--and bodies, were occasionally spotted rushing in the midst of the destruction. That morning, as the current slowed, and the waters receded, the survivors looked out upon the remains of their town:

> Little groups of people are standing around on the hills to the north of Valley Park and looking at the ruins. Many of the glass workers have refused to leave their homes because they have worked for years to save money to buy their residences and have determined to remain with their property. Sheriff Bode said today that he believed some lives had been lost because of the refusal of many of the glass workers, who are foreigners, to be rescued.

1500 to 2000 people were displaced with no employment. A majority of them had worked at the Plate Glass plant, which had been both flooded and consumed by fire. It never reopened.

Years later, the Valley Park Hotel—which had been built by the owners of the Glass Factory high on the hills north of the town, where the waters never reached—itself burned to the ground.

After the flood of 1915, the serenity and prosperity of Valley Park was severely diminished. When the bridge was rebuilt--finished in 1917--a great dedication ceremony was held on and around the bridge, which was a huge event of civic pride. It too was pummeled time after time, flood after flood, until the people of Valley Park were left with a rickety old bridge. For decades, it caused huge traffic problems due to it's narrowness and fragility, and its instability and age made them afraid every time they crossed it. For over ten years the citizens and community leaders of Valley Park argued over what should become of the bridge. On Thursday, July 10th, 1986--the second "County bridge" over the Meramec--was finally blown up to make way for a newer, more efficient highway.

Subsequent floods added to the town's penance. Several businesses left after the 1915 flood, and again after the flood in 1945. The active river-life stopped around this time, as did frequent Railroad service between Valley Park and the city of St. Louis. The Frisco Railroad Bridge still operates, and the Valley Park of today is dominated by a wide expanse of Highway 141 that runs past town, over the exact route that once took wagons and horses across the river, practically concealing the phantom bridge and the lives that clung to it.

Author's Collection

The Question

    The book of Psalms says, "*Thou answeredst them, O Lord our God: thou wast a God that forgavest them, though thou tookest vengeance of their inventions.*" This may have never been more apt than in the place where John Buckner was killed. For nearly it's entire history the town has built itself up just enough to survive--and just when it has seemed to be on the advance, *something* has pulled it back. It is not to say that Valley Park is doomed, so much as it is *haunted*.

    There is a little known tale that the children of Valley Park occasionally tell. In their tale, it is claimed that a man was hung from the bridge in town a long, long time ago. They say at night you can hear his ghost that roams the riverbanks of the Meramec, awaiting the justice he never received; bent on the destruction and ruin of anything that occupies the town. The peaceful, old-timey feeling that one gets from a small town like Valley Park, in relation to it's history; it's shadows; it's ghosts--is rather unsettling. It's residents are either in denial, or totally oblivious to the tragedy and truthfulness of the local history of the last century. The story and destiny of this little hamlet is enigmatic, as its role in St. Louis history has loomed unfulfilled. Ironically, the violence of its past may one day ensure its sad unwanted place. For now, the waters of the Meramec have chosen to sleep, as the story has remained unknown.

Now, the story of John Buckner itself had finally come out from the shadows. As what occurred here in 1894 slowly revealed itself, there was much still to speculate about—yet little to no physical evidence left. The bridge is gone; the homes of John Buckner, Delia Mungo, Justice Hofstetter, and all of the other principals of this story are gone now. All of the witnesses to this crime have died; some surviving to old age mere decades ago. All that is left *is the story*.

Many of us have seen or heard, in the very least a mini-series, a novel, a documentary, or even a rumor--that gives us a few initial tangible images of the hatred and inhumanity of our past. From this, we start off from a clearly defined image in our minds of a different world; our notions of slavery and segregation lead us to initially assume that the only cause of lynching a black man would have to be a simple answer; one that we have all been taught. We know that legacy as well as we know ourselves.

We encounter several different contributing factors other than race alone in this story. It is certain that the hysteria that was created *after* the lynching of John Buckner was biased and flawed, as was most of the racial relations of the United States of that time. Then we have the heightened agitation of the populace of St. Louis, due to the number of crimes in the area in the preceding months and days. Then we have the crime itself. The real question we have to ask was this: *Why was John Buckner lynched?*

The various elements of the typical lynching—the role of rumor and fear, the manhunt tradition, and mob assumptions of absolute guilt-- have been studied since lynching's first notable occurrences in our country. This body of work tells us consistently what the common makeup of the "lyncher" typically is, as well as the typical victim. Such lynchers are themselves put into a category, along with the characteristics of the "mob mind." Lynchers are typically under 30, white, uneducated, and not very financially stable. They usually feel superiority over other races and subscribe to an assumption that all crimes are perpetrated by them. They are described as predators, and the accused as their prey.

The barbarism and torture of such crimes; beatings, mutilation, and a cheerful, carnival atmosphere, are a peculiar feature of the crime, which strangely, we find little of in this case. That peculiarity is traditionally due to racism that the executioners no doubt deeply felt in the lynching practice. We do in fact encounter many elements of racism in this story; aspects of the vernacular used in the story--repeatedly calling Buckner a "negro fiend", and even a "nigger" leap out at us. Also, we know that the hysteria and racism in the days following Buckner's death *nearly sealed the fate of Horace Johnson*. This might make one ponder whether the lynching of John Buckner *was* indeed just another notch on the American belt of racism.

At the same time--we are confronted with other startling aspects of this story, which would seem to contradict the racist label that we typically assign towards the 1890 world. The comments and statements of ordinary citizens lent this subject a rare, insightful glimpse as to what really happened. They gave an unvarnished view of how a person like John Buckner lost his life.

Though I must admit I had approached this story with a pre-supposed sympathy for John Buckner as a victim of lynching, I was aware that he had already been convicted for assaulting a black schoolteacher at the young age of 17; not exactly the typical "victim" of racism.

The more I dug, the less ordinary the case looked for John Buckner. After an initial review, I went back to all of the published material from the weeks after the lynching. I wanted to make sure that I had the clearest picture possible, from every angle, of what type of person John Buckner was.

At the last minute, I found an article published only a few days after Buckner was buried. The following was a special to the St. Louis Republic:

> Later developments in the Buckner case reveal a startling state of affairs in the neighborhood of Valley Park. It seems that the black brute has been a veritable terror to the citizens of that locality. Since such swift and just punishment has been meted out to the

miscreant his past acts are coming to light. Two of his intended victims, who, through fleetness of foot or other fortunate circumstances, managed to escape the brute, have so far come forward and related their experiences. They claim that fear of his vengeance had been the cause of their not complaining before.

Miss Liza Mungo was the first to tell her story. She is a close relative of Mrs. Mungo, his first victim on Tuesday, and her experience was certainly a thrilling one. About three weeks ago, while between Fenton and Valley Park in a thinly settled portion of that hilly country, she was pursued by the scoundrel and followed for a distance of over a mile. She is a lightfooted and active girl, and fear and horror lending speed to her limbs, she ran as if for her life.

Up hill and down dale, through the woods and clearing, sped the frightened girl, and in hot pursuit came the fiend incarnate. But he was doomed to disappointment this time, and the poor child, for she is scarcely 15 years old, reached home in a fearfully exhausted condition. By threats and intimidation Buckner succeeded in frightening the whole family into secrecy, and had not this double outrage terminated his worthless existence nothing would have been known of it to-day.

For those who might reasonably doubt the fidelity of the charge placed around Buckner's neck--here we have the fidelity of a frightened 15-year-old girl, who happened to be the same race as the accused. Moreover, a check with the 1880 census shows us that in fact--she appears to be the oldest daughter of Delia Mungo. The Republic continued:

His other known attempt, or attempts, for in this instance he made the attempt several times, was with a white girl named Mary Schale. She claims that Buckner not once or twice, but repeatedly chased her into her very door in his diabolical attempt to catch and outrage her. When a friend of the girl's was asked why complaint had not been made to the authorities and steps taken to punish the negro, the answer was: "Look at the way criminals are punished in St. Louis County. The man who steals a ham is sent to the penitentiary for 15 or 20 years, while the rapist or murderer is sent to jail for six months to three years, and should we report a case like this and he only get six months or a year what would become of us when he got out again? No, sir; so long as he did not succeed we concluded that discretion was the better part of valor and concluded it better policy to let him run to the end of his rope."

With this, the possibility that Buckner had been framed by angry whites all but vanishes. Though they have been long in their graves, three black women, and two white women accuse him. Their names are Delia Mungo, a wife and mother; Allie Harrison, a nineteen yr. old farmer's daughter; Mary Weaver, a schoolteacher at the Valley Park Colored School; Mary Schale, an unknown girl from the area--and Miss Liza Mungo, a fifteen year old child.

The lynching this morning near Valley Park is not excusable, but is as nearly so as any lawless act can be. There is one class of criminals who would seem to be without the pale even of the law, and they are the brutes who wantonly wreck the whole life and happiness of innocent young girls.

100

There was the *Vox Populi*. John Buckner was a black man. We are thus inclined to believe that his race caused his death. But--if we listen to the voices of the people, perhaps the people who did it, consistently it is said: *it was not his race—but his crime.* This is found in nearly every article and editorial in the city's 5 english newspapers that covered the event. I found in those writings that which is scarcely obtained by newspapers; the raw, primitive honesty of ordinary people, expressed in true feeling.

The question of why Buckner was taken from the authorities and hung is more complex than simply race alone. To answer why, we must first ask--*was Buckner guilty of his crimes?*

A great number of highly regarded authorities on the subject of lynching would have us assume that most, if not all, of those lynched were innocent of their crimes. To believe this in the instance of John Buckner, you would have to deny certain crucial elements of this story. If he were innocent, you would have to believe that (unlike himself) the people who were farmers, business and property owners--who were by all accounts well-regarded law-abiding citizens--chose to lash out at a young black man in an area where other blacks had never been harmed, and, it seems, have never been since, all for no apparent reason. You would have to believe that at least 5 women, some of whom did not even know each other, young and old, 3 of whom were themselves black—were lying, for no apparent reason. You would have to believe that Buckner had been falsely accused, tried, convicted, sentenced, and incarcerated by a Missouri Court for the crime of sexual assault. You would have to believe that he himself had falsely confessed to committing the sexual assault on Mrs. Mungo, again, for no apparent reason.

That is a pretty tall order. Now, if we assume beyond a reasonable doubt that he was guilty of multiple sexual assaults and harassment over a four year period, and if we take into account that his assaults on Mrs. Mungo and Miss Harrison *were only due to his release from the criminal justice system*—we come to our second, most important question; *was the lynching of John Buckner justified?*

In the eyes of the law, it would be simple to answer: NEVER. The lynching would be considered an act of "malice aforethought." It was no accident, and no law would allow civilians to kill a man who was a suspect. It was a crime that ended a man's life, and robbed him of the code of Justice that we live by.

Another view holds that there are times and instances; war, self-defense, disasters--when people have felt that the law of the jungle--the "law of survival"--trumps the law of the civilized world; "a time to kill." If one construed the wilderness of 1894 as a jungle--then one might be inclined to say that the law of the jungle—*the law of survival*-- overruled the law on paper somewhere far from sight, and mind.

The people of St. Louis County may have even seen themselves as heroic for their deed—and indeed this is demonstrated in the comments made in the days immediately after--if you look at it from the standpoint of safety, and survival. They had done what the law seemingly *could not*. If you believe that John Buckner was guilty of his crimes—you might imagine what they themselves might have said. In ending the life of John Buckner, they had relieved the fears of his young female victims, they had punished an evil man for his past offenses to their loved ones, and they had undoubtedly spared an unknown quantity of women and girls the outrages which were fixed in his soul. A time for justice was too long delayed for the sake of innocent young girls, both black and white. The Bible, in the book of Ecclesiastes--says that *there is* a time to kill. If there ever was such a time, the people of St. Louis County believed it was so on the night of January 16th, 1894.

What would motivate so many law-abiding people to commit such an act? After all, John Buckner was lynched by citizens of *both races*; black and white, perhaps because he had committed sexual assaults on a black woman, as well as a white woman. Not only was he convicted of sexual assault before on a black woman, he was accused by two additional victims who had kept quiet until he was safely in the ground.

In everything that was written, documented, printed, editorialized at the time--Buckner posed a continuing threat to the welfare of the people, and the consensus of overwhelming majority opinion states that the lynching was not only justifiable, but was applauded by those of both races.

The Buckner lynching was not an isolated instance of this. In fact, it almost happened on the exact same day in another Missouri town:

A NEGRO RAVISHER IN JAIL.

———

Salisbury, Mo., Jan. 16—About 8 o'clock last night a negro by the name of Phelps assaulted a little colored girl about 5 years old. After accomplishing his purpose he left the city, but during last night he came back to a house in the suburbs of the city and secreted himself. Word came to Marshal Gilchrist where the culprit was hiding, and he arrested him, taking him before Justice Bradley. He acknowledged his guilt. The Justice sent him to jail to await the action of the Grand Jury. At one time *it looked as if the enraged colored people would string the prisoner up*, but better counsel prevailed, so the law will be allowed to take it's course. It is thought the little girl will recover.

There is also some question as to the motivations of the white members of the lynch mob as well. Race aside, there are clues as to why they would be compelled to take Buckner from the authorities and lynch him. For instance, we happen to know that many of them were instrumental in setting up and attending the Vigilance Committee of L. C. Nelson, which met up in the days and weeks after. In an announcement for the committee, known as the "Suburban Safety Association," a mere two days after the lynching, it is made clear the feelings of the common people:

...the young men of the county will organize themselves into a patrol to protect the highways and arrest all suspicious characters, *black or white*.

These young men are farmers' sons, who have sisters and mothers who may be at any time subjected to the danger of insult or assault from the fiends which seem to infest every part of St. Louis County. They are therefore determined to stop the wave of crime that is sweeping their county, if it is possible to do so.

The people of St. Louis County were not mounting an offensive—but rather, in the words of its leader L. C. Nelson, organizing a "scheme of *defense*"— against, as said above, criminals of both the *black and white race*:

Most of the men out my way work away from home and leave their wives and daughters all alone. There is no system of police or deputies to look after the territory. Now we propose to organize and elect officers. Perhaps we can get up a scheme of volunteer guards and import a few cases of Winchesters or double-barreled shotguns. At any rate, the people are coming together Saturday night, and after that, we hope that our homes won't be left entirely unprotected when we're downtown. *That's what this meeting means.*

We tend to take for granted that justice will be served, that criminals will be punished--and that we will be safe. They obviously did not. Perhaps they were simply placed in times and circumstances that we have never been faced with. We may find it hard to believe that in our "modern sensibilities," we have become often intolerant and dismissive of the value of long-held beliefs, traditions, and virtues-- that inspire neighbors to work together, stay in each others lives, and mutually ally and protect themselves despite wealth, or party, or *race*.

One hundred years ago, a different set of rules, both written and unwritten, guided and restricted and repressed citizens in ways that we can never overstate. There was an obvious environment of racial stereotypes that pervaded everything from music, to law, to even the news reporting cited in this story. All one has to do is to ramble through any given week of any newspaper printed near the turn of the century to see racist jokes, racist cartoons, and a racist slant on character and language when it came to black people. Not any harder to assume is that in 1894 a black man was more likely to die from a simple misunderstanding or mistake than almost anyone else.

Nevertheless, no scholar on American History would argue that every black citizen who lived in the age of Jim Crow died a victim of racism, nor as a poster boy for the struggle. No matter what your politics are, most people would agree that a John Buckner was hardly a poster boy for anti-lynching, which is probably why this story has never really been told.

The noted journalist and author Ida B. Wells once said concerning the reporting of lynching, "The Afro-American papers are the only ones which will print the truth." This is a fair question to ask. But it should be noted that a great deal of this story has shown us things which we would never have learned within the context of the accepted versions of Black History, nor even in Mrs. Wells own authoritative works on the subject. In just this one event, there is little to none of the maliciousness found in comparison with other lynchings from other regions. Nor, for that matter, does the Valley Park lynching compare with any of the extremely horrid and racist descriptions detailed in Mrs. Wells 1892 work, *Southern Horrors*, nor her 1900 work *Lynch-Law in America*. If we doubt the validity of the not one, not two--but fully five newspapers that gave coverage to the Valley Park lynching, in detail—then must we not also doubt the lynching statistics that form the foundation of African-American history?

Numerous authors and scholars of this subject point out that all major sources of the names, dates, and information on lynching--derive primarily from newspapers. Even the studies done by prominent Civil Rights organizations in the last century have compiled their lists of lynching victims from one central source--*newspaper reports*. This is what I have in a large part presented here. In addition, any true student of Black History will openly acknowledge that Ida Wells was herself *a newspaper journalist*. If the assertion is made that the research compiled here about this incident is faulty, misleading, corrupted, false--then so it must be said of our notion of African-American history.

One might ask--*was the story accurately reported?* It is true that black men and women at the time largely had no voice in the so-called "white" press, and, therefore, the odds are that a black man would not have been fairly or accurately represented in the press journalism of 1894. However, there is an equal assumption that if these were indeed times so tainted that journalism was little more than a propaganda machine for racist attitudes--which only portray blacks as being contrary, cowardly, insipid, and inhuman—that assumption would be at odds with a story in which a black woman is described as "refined, both in manners and appearance." Even the Buckner family is described as "fairly respected and considered good enough" in the community. Not only are blacks described at times as "respected" or "intelligent"—but most ironically—they are also described in every single account as among the protagonists who lynched Buckner. The *St. Louis Republic* stated it simply:

There was no color line drawn.

One of Buckner's victims was an aged colored woman and some of those who assisted in his execution belong to his race. The indignant citizens regarded him as a wild beast and destroyed him.

Then the question arises: *just who were the African-Americans that are repeatedly described as part of the lynch mob?*

From census figures, maps, and descriptions of Valley Park, we know that there were a handful of black families who did live in the area. In the area of the incidents, there were but two--the Buckner's, and the Mungo's. We must remember-- that it was young Lizzie Mungo who had been harassed and chased by Buckner around the area of Valley Park. We must remember that it was Albert Mungo, who, together with William Harrison, first summoned the chase after Buckner personally on

horseback. It was his wife, Delia Mungo--
Buckner's first victim--who witnesses said
identified Buckner at the bridge, as he stood bound
with rope:

> Mrs. Mungo, in conversation with a
> Post-Dispatch reporter, said: "When I heard that
> Buckner had tackled Allie Harrison I ran down
> the road to meet my husband and told him what
> the fiend had done to me. He did not get excited
> but sent me into the house to get a few dollars. I
> brought him the money and he turned his horse
> around and drove to Valley Park. He did not
> come home again until after 3 o'clock."

The attack itself occurred on Mrs. Mungo at around
two or three in the afternoon, as stated in the
account. According to her story, "he seized her, and
for many minutes they engaged in a struggle that
was abusive and almost deathlike... dragged her
torn, bleeding, half-senseless form into the
neighboring brush and carried out his purpose."
She then was left in a "semi-conscious" state.
Buckner then had to walk to the Harrison farm—
wait and then assault Allie Harrison, and we know
from Mrs. Mungo's own words that she did not
even tell her husband until *after* this time. We
would have to assume then that the above "3
o'clock" of Al Mungo's return home refers to 3
AM, in the middle of the night. That would mean
that Al Mungo was not only the first to go after
Buckner that afternoon, but that he did not come
home for at least *ten hours*. He would have
returned home just as the lynching party was on its
way towards Valley Park with John Buckner.

Out of all of those who may have lived in

Valley Park, one could say that Albert Mungo would have had the most understandable motive for killing John Buckner; his daughter had been accosted and chased on several occasions, and now his wife had been beaten, raped, and left on the side of the road. That might explain why Albert got money before leaving. Strangely, Mrs. Mungo states that he left for "Valley Park." There was no officer of the law there. Valley Park was, however, where the mob materialized that evening. We know that there were some "negroes" present at the scene of Buckner's capture by the mob, who reportedly "wanted to string him to the first tree." The St. Louis Globe-Democrat also confirmed this in its description:

> The negro (Buckner) pleaded continually for mercy and volunteered the statement that he had not succeeded in ravishing Miss Harrison, although he had done so with Mrs. Mungo. This, however, did not have the desired effect upon the mob, which contained a large colored contingent, and the doomed man was hurried on to his place of execution.

It is pure speculation, but Al Mungo might possibly have been among them. He came home just in time so that Delia could positively identify him to the mob and attest to his crimes. Another clue may be in the following curious statement by Valley Park resident J. S. McMurtrie:

> The feeling in the community is, that if the lynchers got the right man (of that there seems to be little doubt) they did right in stringing him up. The Mungo family was a respectable, industrious one and was well

thought of in the neighborhood. They have lived there for many years and were never involved in any offensive dealings.

The statement of Mrs. Mungo hints at something more, without really saying it. By putting the pieces together of statements made by eyewitnesses, reporters, and Mrs. Mungo—there is a valid question as to what role both of the Mungo's played in Buckner's fate. What we do know--is that shortly after Albert came back home, at 3 AM--both she and him left together for the Meramec River Bridge.

An anonymous reader wrote this to the Post-Dispatch a few days after the lynching:

> THERE was no color line in the lynching of Ravisher Buckner at Valley Park. The victims of the brutal negro were a white woman and a colored woman. Both whites and blacks took part in the lynching bee and it is alleged that nineteen out of twenty citizens of St. Louis County of all colors and conditions indorse the action of the mob. The locality is in the heart of civilization. This case may be taken as the fairest possible indication of the temper of all the people toward criminals of the Buckner type. There seems no hope of stopping lynching until crimes against women are stopped.

We must remember, no matter what race John Buckner might have belonged to, we must first remember what was his crime. We must look through the lens of 1894, and listen to the common voices. If we, in the present day had no real police presence in our neighborhood, our county, and these people were let out on the street, and repeated offenses--to young women that we knew personally--we must consider what our reaction might have been.

As I was researching this story--the kidnapping, rape, and murder of 6 year old Cassandra "Casey" Williamson touched the people of Valley Park, and the entire St. Louis area. Johnny Johnson, a 26 year old drifter and ex-convict, befriended Casey's parents--both residents of Valley Park--and, after spending two nights with them, took off early on the morning of July 26, 2002 hand in hand with little Casey, barefoot and still in her nightgown, as her parents slept. Johnson walked her the few blocks through town, then carried her piggyback to an obscure trail towards the Meramec River. There he entered through some abandoned tunnels that led into the bowels of the old Plate Glass Factory, destroyed in the 1915 flood, but was still partially intact.

There, in one of the old ovens, he beat her with a brick, attempted to sexually assault her, and then crushed her skull with a large rock when she resisted his actions. He left her to die in the dark oblivion of the old glass factory, buried under a pile of rocks. Johnson then went down the short distance to the banks of the river, and washed the blood off of himself there in the waters of the Meramec, a short 700 feet east of the 141 bridge. He then walked back up the bluff and went back into town as though nothing had happened, going back to get some cigarettes. He was caught, tried, and convicted to die for his actions.

We must ask ourselves, what if there was rampant crime, and little to no real police presence to protect us? In a hypothetical situation, what if we had seen, time after time, people like Johnson go through the system, only to be let out to repeat the offences? What if Casey had been raped in 1894, or Mrs. Mungo and Miss Harrison in 2002?

At some point, we have to be honest with ourselves as to what our reaction would have been if 100 of our closest family and friends were going to seriously deal with Johnson after he had kidnapped, raped, and murdered little Casey. Would we be so patient and calm and ready for the ponderous wheels of Justice to take their course, or would we be tempted to go take care of that monster on our terms—especially if he had done so before in our neighborhood? We know of course that Johnson is white--*but it matters little to those who would exact Justice on Johnny Johnson what color he is*. His crimes are colorless. The same might be said with John Buckner.

We of course know that the circumstances surrounding Buckner's death was the exception and not the rule when it came to lynchings in American history. The majority of those lynched *after* January 17, 1894 were done so for more wholly unjustifiable reasons; deeply felt racist attitudes, and intolerance for any form of social equality between the inherent rights of white men and that of black men. It is important that the reader understand that no matter what the details of this single event leads one to believe, it does not overshadow in any way the terrible blot on our nation's history that racism has caused; rioting, lynching, slavery, segregation, and all of the single instances of injustice against black people which comprise 400 years of indignity.

Perhaps it is fitting to ask the question--*if Buckner had been white, would he have been lynched for the crimes he had committed?*

Simply a look at statistics will reveal the probability that he would have. One of the largest historical inaccuracies that has been perpetuated in contemporary times is that lynching was always a crime committed exclusively against blacks. There are numerous sources throughout the last two centuries that teach us otherwise. In fact, until the 1890's, lynching really had no specific race as a target. One of the earliest authorities on the subject was Professor John Walter Gregory, Chair at the University of Glasgow. In 1925, he wrote the following of the practice, "It was not originally directed against the Negro, and was freely used against *white* criminals, and even against *white women*, of whom 23 have been lynched." He cited another example, stating that in 1885, "...106 white people were lynched as against 78 negroes." The year before, 160 whites had been lynched in the United States.

According to another source, of the approximate 300 lynchings in America between 1840 and 1860, less than 10 percent of the victims were black. By the last decade of the nineteenth century, whites still at times barely outnumbered blacks as victims of lynch mobs. In Missouri in 1896, six white men were lynched at different times, and at various places. *No blacks were lynched in Missouri that year.* According to the twelfth census as late as 1900, the number of whites lynched in the state of Missouri comprised a total of 53.84 percent, as opposed to "negroes"--at 46.15 percent.

Furthermore, murder and sexual and physical assaults on women were the main cause of lynching. Rape was a crime considered at the time worse than murder. Both before and after 1894, men were lynched in the state for much less aggreivous offences. John Swinney, a white man, was lynched at Arrow Rock, Missouri in 1873 for arson. Peter Kessler, also white, was lynched in Fulton, Missouri on August 15, 1873 for "horse stealing and threats." Four months before Buckner was lynched, a white man named Redmond Burke was lynched for simply beating his wife. In 1897, three white men were lynched in the state, for the lesser offences of larceny and arson. That year, only *one* black man was lynched in Missouri; Erastus Brown, for the more serious crime of rape. As Professor John Walter Gregory put it, *"The defective administration of the law has been the chief cause and excuse for lynching... Lynching was started owing to the need in the primitive conditions of life back in the back country for quick, effective punishment."*

Both national and state statistics, as well as those put out by the NAACP and other organizations--support the view that race did not seem to be a factor in lynching until about the mid-1890's, when the statistics began to shift, and the number of white lynchings dropped to single digits. It was not until then that authors such as Ida B.

Wells began to assert the racial and regional aspects of the practice. It is naive to assume that race did not play a part in the lynching of John Buckner, but--equally, it is unwise to assume that racism erases the crimes for which Buckner was hanged, *a crime for which at the time perpetrators of both races were often hanged.*

We are separated from these people and events because of what has transpired all of the hours and days and years since 5 AM January 17th, 1894. Our world lends little to theirs. To really take a stab at the motivations of the mob, we have to step back from the present day, into a world that is much different than we really can conceive. One hundred years ago, people "on the prairie" often dealt with important issues on their own, or with the assistance of their nearest neighbors and relatives only. They did not live with television, radio, or the Internet, and only occasionally had access to books.

Often, people's words and actions took on a more dependable and definite meaning. More than today, people openly spoke what they believed, and lines were more clearly drawn. In one way, this made people of different backgrounds more intolerant of each other as their diverse cultures, attitudes, and beliefs clashed. This continues to the present day. That has been the experiment of America, both in freeing people and in enslaving people--that people are forced to live together though they be composed of opposite extremes; between Democrat and Republican; between Rich and Poor; between Black and White.

Somehow, in the midst of all of these

divisions, common people found their own ways to live their lives together, despite their situation. In the case of John Buckner, the feelings of the people who lynched him are a mystery.

The best guess comes from the voices of the people who were there. The following is an editorial that was written a day or two after the lynching by a county citizen:

THE BUCKNER LYNCHING.

The lynching of the negro, John Buckner, for brutal outrages committed upon two women yesterday at Valley Park brought mob law to the gates of St. Louis.

Such violations of law and order as are represented by the hanging of this human brute seem inevitable. No appeal to public sentiment, respect for authority or love of good government is strong enough to prevent them. The nature of the crime arouses passionate resentment of the beasts of men and urges them to desperate measures for the protection of their homes and families. The lynching method is the worst method because it overthrows all the principles of just law enforcement and sound government. It is doubtful if it has a deterrent effect upon other brutes. It undoubtedly has a brutalizing effect upon a community. But it is the method seized upon by unreasoning mobs and it is so far endorsed by public sentiment that it is vain to expect the vindication of law by the punishment of lynchers.

Lynch law can never be justified, but

there is this much excuse for the lynching of Buckner. He had been guilty of a double crime of the most cruel nature. He had just been released from the penitentiary for a similar crime. It was natural that the neighbors of the outraged women should conclude in their horror and indignation that there was no safety for helpless women as long as this vicious brute lived. His death was a good riddance but it is a pity that the law was violated to accomplish it.

This story poses somewhat new territory in the retrospect view of the "jim crow" era, one that seldom *if ever* is written about. The notion of active black participation in a lynching leaves a strange taste in mouth because this is not just revisionist history we are toying with here--but racial revisionist history, which we are often not willing to explore *or correct.*

In the final analysis, there is much more to this story than what one might expect. John Buckner is not the victim we would have expected him to be. This was by no account a good man with a clean record. The people who lynched John Buckner are maybe not whom we might have expected them to be. Perhaps they seem *too reasonable to fit with our preconceived notions.* Perhaps--*perhaps*--our preconceived notions are *wrong.*

Despite our cynicism, the fact that Buckner was incarcerated for 3 years for assaulting a *black* woman should tell us that there was indeed some measure of justice for black citizens who were victims of crime. The fact that an elderly white woman came to the defense of a young accused black man named Horace Johnson speaks volumes also. The words of those involved, and of the many St. Louis County residents who felt compelled to write down their thoughts make it plain to us. We cannot, and should not, ignore them any longer. Perhaps the rampant racism and injustice label that we place on all of our ancestors is poorly deserved. The fact that we look for such racism says as much about *us* as it does about them, if not more. Perhaps this too emanates from a flawed view of our history which we should re-evaluate and re-examine, case by case. We owe all of our ancestors that much.

Perhaps some will speculate that the newspapers embellished or lied, that the witnesses had an agenda, and that most of this story is simply fiction. So are so many unsupported claims made of other times, places, and people in our past. Context and perspective put a different edge on all of our views, and thus must be said of our view of history, and of interpretation of words and deeds. Perhaps the big lesson here--is that we ought not to become complacent with what we are taught as though *it were the complete picture of truth.* Nonetheless, it is healthy that this discussion--this argument--does indeed happen in the first place. It is our right to do so, and perhaps we should.

The people of Missouri have a reputation for toughness, plain-talk, and common sense. The state which gave birth to Mark Twain, Harry Truman, Jesse James, and to the legends of Stagger Lee and Frankie and Johnny--has for it's state motto the Latin phrase "*SALUS POPULI SUPREMA LEX ESTO*"--which means "The welfare of the people is the supreme law." The lynching of John Buckner stands apart from both the history we have been taught and from the morality and law of modern society that we rarely question. The citizens of St. Louis County, both black and white, who lynched John Buckner are from one view *heroes*, yet, at the same time, *antiheroes*. In the final analysis, it should be pointed out that a man died at the hands of other men, and it was--in the eyes of the law--*a crime*. A crime was committed when the prisoner was taken from the authorities. A crime was committed when the prisoner was denied the right to a trial. A crime was committed when the ordinary citizens of St. Louis County executed him. By the standards of the law, those who did the deed are just as contemptible, and just as guilty, if not more so--than John Buckner. By Missouri standards, it is in the light of his crimes, and in the eminent threat he posed *to the welfare of the people* of St. Louis County that the lynching of John Buckner was justified.

> *Buckner's crime had been an awful one. It included the third of a similar nature and proved that this character was that of a brute. Swinging so in the cool morning breeze, with the river's bright waters rippling merrily over innumerable pebbles below, the administrators of such summary justice were fully assured that at least he would not further disturb the peace of their pleasant homes. The scenes of the night previous to the tragic enactment of unwritten moral law, were fully as appalling as the tragic climax itself. Never before had the residents of Valley Park, Manchester, and the surrounding territory evinced any desire to intercept the ordinary course of justice. They had lived along*

in peace, taken the illegalities of men as they came, with the assurance that ordinary legal processes would fully avenge them. Yesterday however, and the night before, the calm was broken. Justice could not be waited for, and Buckner's death was the outcropping of such anxious fury as knew no bounds and process other than that of speed.

-The St. Louis Republic January 18, 1894.

GIRLS WANTED ON THE MUSQUODOBOIT RIVER

Author's Collection

Shadows Never Rest

When I made the trip down to Valley Park
for the first time, I didn't know what would be there
for me to find. A tiny strip mall stands where the
club and boathouses once stood along the river
bluff. There is nothing special or unique about the
spot. Indeed, it looks much like any other
unordinary place where consumers buy things that
they probably don't need, only to return home
unsatisfied.

Beyond the store parking lot around back is
the spot where Mrs. Mungo had stood and identified
John Buckner. A few hundred yards to the east, one
can still see trains crossing the Frisco Railroad
Bridge, where passengers riding to St. Louis first
caught the sight of a man hanging from the wagon
bridge. Sitting in my car, there in the shadows
where a truss of that bridge had once stood, I looked
out on the stretch of highway that overlooks the
Meramec. I realized that the bridge looked not so
much as a bridge at all, but rather a long, flat
concrete slab, concealing the mighty waters that

rushed beneath it. Unlike Ford's Theatre, Dealey Plaza, the Lorraine Motel, or Ground Zero--there is no map that marks this historic place. There is no Park Service; no Historic Register to designate this spot, nor share this tale of our history. Like the bridge, the story became a casualty of time.

When the 1915 flood destroyed the Glass factory under six-feet of water, the owners declared bankruptcy, and sold the entire mess at auction for the sum of $400,000. While the factory was being repaired, in February 1916--the structure burned to the ground--started by coke burners used to heat the building during construction. For nearly a century, nothing was left but a maze of tunnels that led down to the underground chambers of the old site. After the recent murder of Casey Williamson at the site in 2002, the remnants of the structure were uprooted, and is now nothing more than a huge dirtpile stretching along the banks of the Meramec.

Before the Plate Glass Factory opened, a mere 300 citizens made up Valley Park--then known as Meramec Station. Not even a decade later, the population soared to 2,100. After the flood, nearly 2,000 homeless moved away. In many ways, the Glass Factory was the life and death of Valley Park, Missouri. The same could be said of the Meramec. Most assuredly, Valley Park is destined for another distant chapter, as yet unknown to us. It may yet become the resort and industrial center it once it was destined to be. For now--it is a sort of ghost town. *If there is a spirit that roams the Meramec--he giveth, and he taketh away.*

When I got out of my car, and walked

behind the row of stores down towards Marshall Road and the Meramec, I half expected to see a sign, or a plaque, or anything that denoted the history of the spot. A part of me had a naive notion from the very beginning—that, when I came to Valley Park--that I would come to a place that would reveal something, a shred of evidence, a rotten cord of petrified rope, a postcard, a dusty torn photograph, perhaps even a kind old griot, living nearby in some dingy old boathouse that might have survived--who would lend something tangible through some unbelievable but familiar story.

Standing there under the bridge that is now US Highway 141; there is an almost surreal normalcy and nothingness to the spot. Cars and trucks speed by overhead, and occasionally a lone boy will fish down in the sandy pilings. Strewn amongst the rocks was only the rotten carcass of a dog, withering away beneath the sun. The glory of Valley Park's past is nowhere to be seen, vanished along with the descendants of the Buckner and Mungo families, who also seem to have simply disappeared. The landings, canoe rentals, and the happy faces along the Meramec River have vanished from memory. The word Meramec itself is a mysterious word, supposedly of Algonquin origin. The literal translation is " The River of Ugly Fishes"--but is commonly known to fishermen as "Ugly Water." (No one seems to know what it really means.) At the Valley Park Library, beneath dozens of scrapbooks lies an unfinished draft of an early history of the town of Valley Park. In it, the word Meramec is defined as "the Water of Death."

I waited down there for hours--waiting there

for something to change--but it didn't. Nothing happened. No one seems to go there anymore. I could see as I walked down to the river the trail of large boulders, half-embedded in the ground, exactly where the bridge had stood; where both bridges had once stood. Up ahead, I could see the bulldozers clearing the mounds of dirt over the last remnants of the Glass Factory. When I was standing there alone--it was then that I was struck with the denial and silence of a lost past. The active river-life is gone, Valley Park is smaller, and 141 is there as if it never even happened. Most people are on their way somewhere else, far from here, and don't even realize that they have crossed a bridge at all, of which now it is not even a shadow.

But right there in that inglamorous spot, a community took a man and hung him. A few miles from Chrysler, The Train Museum, and Six Flags, and in their time they might not have been so different from us. They had their entertainment and recreation, and they tried to be both law abiding and human. They were vigilant and they were proud. To many then, they had drawn a line. This was their home, and *that* was their center. They did not feel like murderers, as we, in our modern sensibilities, tend to view them. On a January night in 1894, a group of citizens committed a crime in the name of Justice. By doing so, they became a part of our history, and either willingly or unwillingly, a whisper and a secret in the shadow of Judge Lynch. They had taken their community back, on their terms--until the mighty waters of the Meramec took it from them.

The citizens of Valley Park say—and

126

we believe them, because they ought to know—
that their town is a pleasant place to live in; that
it is a great town; that the word "progressive"
will head a majority of the ballots cast whenever
a vote is taken on a question of incorporation;
that it is a business center, the heart of
manufacturing industry, the home of advanced
educational ideals, the bullseye when you aim at
healthful pastime, and the hotbed in which
prosperity is propagated.

-History of St. Louis County. 1910.

The small community of Valley Park of
today is almost entirely secure from it's haunting
past. Beyond the old timers and locals that
remember the stories of their grandfathers lies a self
fulfilled denial; behind the memories of floods and
personal reflections, there is something that never
seems to surface. The rumor that a black man had
been lynched was by the early 1960's not taken that
seriously, and after the high school students that had
continued to spread it had moved on and gotten
married and grown into their own families, it
became largely forgotten, lost in the shuffle of petty
gossip that accumulates over time.

What remains are the vague notations that
have slipped their way into only a few obscure
publications about the history of St. Louis, and that
of the history and settlement of black people in the
area. The minute references that they make leave a
huge question--waiting to be asked, and asked
again, and to not be forgotten, where *for now* it
seems to have been assigned. This is a story that--
for many St. Louisans--has not been heard.
Something this real, and horrible, and forgotten for

so long *pleads* to be seen. After all, this was not in Mississippi, well outside of our comfort zone. This was not some far off unreachable time and place that we cannot understand. This was here, at home—on the sparkling waters of the Meramec River.

The grave of John Buckner lies in a valley just a half-mile past a Quicktrip, nestled between the chain-link fences of neighboring backyards. The Triune Baptist Cemetery for Colored People is a barren overgrown lot of unmarked graves along the curve in the road. Only a poorly painted sign rises out of the earth, which bears the Cemetery's name. Sadly, this too is a place that says nothing to those who pass by, and have no idea what lies beneath the surface.

When I started out that Sunday morning in late summer to find the town of Valley Park, I descended the crest of a hill and there--before I knew it, I had already passed the Meramec River, and within a matter of a second or two had traced the shadow of the bridge that was gone. Indeed, the sometimes angry and sometimes serene waters of Valley Park have washed away the stain of blood from a demolished bridge, but it continues to haunt those who know what heritage they daily step over. For the rest of my life when I cross a bridge--I may pause, and wonder what stories are buried there, as with the Old Wagon Bridge across the Meramec, where the unknown ghost of John Buckner still lingers.

Sources

The Alton Telegraph newspaper. April 1836.

The Liberator newspaper. June 25, 1836.

The Memphis Daily Commercial newspaper. May 17, 1894.

The St. Louis Chronicle newspaper. January 12-19, 1894.

The St. Louis Globe-Democrat newspaper. January 7-23, 1894. July 2-4, 1917.

The St. Louis Observer newspaper. March-April 1836.

The St. Louis Post-Dispatch newspaper. January 17-28, 1894. July 2-4, 1917. July 11, 1986. photo.

The St. Louis Republic newspaper. January 11-19, 1894.

The St. Louis Star newspaper. January 5-19, 1894. August 23, 1915.

The St. Louis Star-Sayings newspaper. January 17-19, 1894.

The Valley Park Sun newspaper. April 10, 1909.

The West County Journal newspaper. August 19, 1981.

Frank Leslie's Weekly. September 30, 1882.

History of St. Louis County, Missouri. William H. Thomas. 1911.

King James Bible. Book of Job. Book of Psalms. Book of Ecclesiastes. 1611.

Lynch-Law:An Investigation into the History of Lynching in the United States. James E. Cutler. 1905.

The Menace of Colour; A Study of the Difficulties Due to the Association of White & Coloured Races. J. W. Gregory. 1925.

Pitzman's Map of 1878 of St. Louis and St. Louis County. St. Louis Main Public Library.

The Red Record:Tabulated Statistics and Alleged Causes of
Lynching in the United States.
Wells-Barnett, Ida B. 1895.

Register of Inmates. Missouri State Penitentiary. 1889. Volume P.

Report to the Nation on the Situation in Mississippi. President John
F. Kennedy. 1963.

Southern Horrors: Lynch Law in All Its Phases. Wells-Barnett, Ida
B. 1892.

Thirty Years of Lynching in the United States. NAACP. 1919.

United States Federal Census. 1880-1900. Bonhomme, St. Louis
County.

Valley Park in 1909. Valley Park Library.

*With special thanks to the Valley Park Library, The St. Louis Main
Public Library, The Missouri State Archives in Jefferson City, and to
Mrs. Marlene Hedrick.*

Joseph Wood lives and works in St. Louis, Missouri,
and hopes that this work will inspire new generations to
explore
the living past. His children, Vincent and Je'Bria, are *his*
inspiration,
and are his most treasured assets.

-For Sandra, Alfred, and Qiana